POWER GAMES
OF *Life*

POWER GAMES OF *Life*

SUHAS INAMDAR

PARTRIDGE
A Penguin Company

To order additional copies of this book, contact
Partridge India
000 800 10062 62
www.partridgepublishing.com/india
orders.india@partridgepublishing.com

I dedicate this book to my parents,
who have taught me how to be happy always.

CHAPTER 1

1962—MUMBAI

The school bell rang as all the students hurried to enter the school. They did not want to get punished for coming late. The scene was full of energy, as the students of all ages ran across the ground to reach their respective classrooms. It was an everyday scene, anyway.

Pankaj Shastri reached his class fast enough to keep his bag under the desk and rest for a while before the class began. Pankaj loved to be in time always. For a student of 5th grade, this was an unusual quality. Even when he went out with his family, he got ready before everyone else, so that others didn't waste their time waiting for him.

The class teacher arrived and the buzzing class became silent at once.

The teacher started teaching the lesson and observed that Srikant Joglekar was not concentrating in the class. She had a feeling that he was doing some mischief when her back was towards the class. To confirm her doubt, she abruptly turned towards the students while writing on the black board. And she caught him. He was talking to the students around him as if he was telling them a story. And the three boys around him were happily listening to him.

She asked Srikant to stand up and asked him what was going on.

Srikant looked around, took a deep pause and said, 'Nothing teacher. I was only clarifying a doubt with them on the subject you taught yesterday.'

The teacher was more puzzled than angry. 'Why should you discuss with others about what I taught yesterday, while I am teaching a new topic today? And why did you not interrupt me yesterday, while I was teaching?'

Srikant looked at all the students and then said, 'Well teacher, you were teaching so well yesterday that I did not want to interrupt your flow of teaching. Had I asked you my doubt, it would have wasted precious time of all the students in class.'

The teacher's ego was satisfied that her 'flow of teaching' was very good yesterday. In that feeling of satisfaction, she asked Srikant to sit down and continued teaching.

In the lunch interval, children were having lunch from their Tiffin boxes under a tree in the school playground.

Amit Saxena was looking out of the school gate and thinking something, as if calculating. Vikram Suri asked him, what he was looking at.

Amit said, 'Look at the Guava fruit vendor outside. He is selling Guavas at 5 paise each. Assuming that he sells 25 Guavas in a day, he earns a Savva Rupaya. Let us also assume that his investment is zero, as he must have plucked these fruits from a tree somewhere nearby for free. So, he makes Rs. 37.50 per month and . . .'

Vikram interrupted him and said, 'Amit, why are you calculating all this? He is a poor fellow, who did not get proper education and that is why he is there. However, if he works hard, he can be selling more fruits, and then open a fruit stall of his own and finally have a stall in front of each school selling his fruits.'

Pankaj and Srikant were amazed at the thought processes of their friends in the group. Soon the bell rang and the children hurried to their classrooms to commence the boring afternoon periods.

*   *   *

1967—Mumbai

The SSC results were out and the school had performed well. 83% of its students had passed in first class and 12% in second class. The boys were discussing about their future plans as to what they wanted to become in life.

Amit said as if dreaming, 'I want to earn a lot of money. There is no fun in life without money. If I am required to work very hard for that, I am prepared to do that.'

Pankaj said to Amit, 'Well, money alone cannot bring you happiness. The quality of life also has to be good. There are many things in life other than just earning money.'

Vikram thought for a while and said, 'You both are right. One needs a certain minimum amount of money to be happy, but still money is not everything. I read recently that somewhere in Europe, a millionaire has donated all his wealth to charity and took up the job of a school teacher. And apparently he is now leading a happy life. He does not bother about taxes, business competition etc.'

Srikant had been listening to this conversation all the while. He said in a resigned tone, 'What is the use of you guys making any plans? Everything in life does not happen exactly the way you want it to happen. You need to keep making compromises all through your life . . .'

Some more friends joined them and the discussions drifted towards which college to join and which stream to join. Of course, engineering and medicine were the hot favorites among many. There were quite a few who even had a dream of going to USA. While they were not very clear at this stage as to what they would do there, they had a feeling that the quality of life in USA would be much better than that in India. There were some students who had an established family business like paint shop, or garment store . . . for them the choice was very clear, just to take forward the family business.

One day they went for a mela held in an open ground near their locality. The exhibition had various rides like the giant wheel, roller coaster, 'Maut ka Kuaan' etc., stalls of various household items, toys and also snacks. It was a festive atmosphere there as the exhibition was full of children and their parents. The four friends were also very excited to visit the exhibition, which they had planned to visit since one week.

They had a lot of fun in the exhibition. They had carried money given by their parents and spent the money in military style, which meant everyone spent for himself. However, there was some difference in the way they spent their money. Vikram spent the money on buying books on Science quiz and General Knowledge. He was interested in knowing the mysteries of science. Physics was his favorite subject. That is why, on his birthdays, he asked his parents to give him books. Amit did not buy much. He believed in saving the money and spending it for a better purpose in future. He had a discreet desire to open a bank account and deposit some money in it. He always wondered from where the banks got money to pay interest. Also, he was fascinated by the owner of a corner store near his house, who bought the groceries from the whole sale market at cheap rates and sold it at higher rates with handsome profits. Srikant spent all the money in eating various items like Bhel Puri, Pav Bhaji, Ice cream etc. He was a connoisseur of food. He could not resist the temptation of good food. He always kept a track of good food joints around his house. He used to give free advice to his friends on the best place to get Paani Puri or Masala Dosa or Guajarati Thali. Pankaj played some rides and donated rest of the money among the beggars outside the entrance. He had a very soft heart. He could not see any one around him in distress. He wanted to help others as much as possible. He valued money very much and believed that real satisfaction came from helping those in need. They all returned happily from the exhibition fully tired.

They all studied very hard for the next two years. Vikram's parents had enrolled him in a reputed coaching institute by name Agarwal classes. He used to study diligently and got good marks in all the exams conducted on a weekly basis. He used to share the entire study material with his friends Amit, Srikant and Pankaj. They spent many nights studying together, clarifying one another's doubts and in the process strengthening their knowledge of the subject. While Amit and Pankaj made some serious efforts to improve their knowledge, Srikant somehow was not that keen. He searched for opportunities to stop studying. However, one good thing was that he did not disturb others while they were studying.

Finally, it so happened that only Vikram got admission in an engineering college while Amit and Pankaj took admission in B.Sc. Srikant opted for B.A as that was the only course left for him. They had an eventful get together one evening to mark the important milestone, of completing school life, and also to wish Vikram all the very best for his engineering course. He was going to be away from them for next 5 years studying in Regional Engineering College, Trichy.

*   *   *

1971

Srikant was going through the fresh employment news journal to check if there were any new vacancies for B.A graduates. Ever since he passed his graduation last year, it was his routine activity to wait for Tuesday, when the new edition of Employment News journal was released. He sat in the Gulzar café and ordered his second tea while he gazed through the pages, almost with a mindset that there would be nothing in it for him this week too. And he was right. He started wondering about what would happen to the topper of his class. What career plan would he make for himself? Was there any big career awaiting a BA topper? If there was none, then what was the use of such a degree course, which does not guarantee a job after completion? He had heard somewhere that a brilliant student can find his own way, whichever field he chooses. But currently his imagination was failing him in identifying any such lucrative career path for a BA graduate

Meanwhile Amit had completed his B.Sc and joined a Business Management college in Surat. It was a private college and his father had to borrow loan to fund his education. Amit had already completed his first year now and was pretty much interested in studies. He stood third in the class in the first year final exams. He was the most visible personality in the college in any event, be it cultural or educational or inter-college competitions. Amit's professors were quite surprised about the solutions proposed by Amit on the case studies on various subjects. The solutions were not necessarily drawn from the textbooks and were highly practical. It surprised them as to how this student, who does not have any work experience, could come up with such clever answers.

Pankaj had joined M.Sc course in the same college and was very much interested in pursuing further studies. He always felt that knowledge alone brings power to a person. He was always willing to learn new subjects and apply the knowledge gained through books. He dreamt of doing PhD after finishing his master's degree. One of his fantasies was to acquire so many degrees that the number of letters in his qualification would be more than that of his name.

Vikram was studying hard for his final exams of engineering. He had been an average student in the engineering college during all the semesters. He would promise himself to obtain better marks in next semester, after the results of every semester were declared. Nevertheless, he was a sincere student and never indulged in any kind of wrong activities in college. He knew that campus interviews were held every year in the college by reputed companies looking for the brightest students. Many of the students would get a job offer in their hands before they get their degree certificate. He wanted to be one of them.

CHAPTER 2

1972

Vikram was very happy today as his results were declared and he had passed engineering in first class. His happiness knew no bounds at the thought of calling himself an engineer. It was a dream come true for him. His parents were also extremely happy at their son's achievement. Every father in this world becomes happy to see his son's achievement, even if they were more than his own achievements.

There were extended celebrations in his house. All the near and dear ones were coming to his house for congratulating him and wishing him good luck for the future. He was feeling like a celebrity and was enjoying every moment of it.

His old friends Amit, Srikant and Pankaj also came to meet him. They had a delicious lunch prepared by his proud mother in his house. They were discussing on the terrace after the lunch. It was a cloudy day so the breeze was much more effective in making a pleasant environment.

Amit said, 'What next Vikram? Shall we start a business? A job gives you only a limited income every month. But you can earn unlimited money only in business.'

Vikram was startled at this unexpected invitation.

He said, 'No way, Amit! First I need to get some work experience. You would be taking a big risk to start a business with me, when I am raw from college with no professional experience.'

Pankaj interrupted, 'Come on Vikram, why do you have a problem when he is ok with the idea? After all, in business, a partner with trust is more important than a partner with knowledge.'

Srikant was quietly listening to the ongoing conversation.

Vikram thought for a while and said, 'Money is not the only thing in life. I need to have job satisfaction. I need to always feel that I am utilizing my full potential. I want to see that as an engineer I am useful to my family, my company, my community, my nation and the world . . .'

The discussion had suddenly gone in a highly philosophical note.

Vikram continued, 'We come into this world and we depart. Does it make any difference to anyone around us? Of what use is our existence, if we are not able to improve the world around us? There is something called a . . .'

Amit interrupted, 'Vikram, all this talk of yours is only good for books and cinemas. In reality, what you need for happiness is money and plenty of money. Without money, you will be left nowhere. No one would even look at you. Look around you and you will see that only the rich people in this world get all the respect and attention. Poor people live every day and die every day.'

As if to make his point more clear, he suddenly looked down from the terrace and saw one rikshaw puller carrying a huge load of boxes in his cycle rikshaw. He was struggling to pedal the rikshaw as it was upward climb and the load was too heavy. He was sweating yet pulling on.

Amit said, 'Do you think he has no noble ideas? He has, undoubtedly. The very fact that he is using a cycle rikshaw for his living shows that he wants to live a dignified life. He could have become a thief easily. That would have been far easier. Yet he chose to lead a hard life and earn money in a righteous manner. But what has his nobility given him? Only a confirmed meal for two times a day? Well, life is much more than that.'

Pankaj was listening to both sides intently and said, 'Guys, let us not convert our exchange of ideas into a fight. Money does play a role in our life but beyond money there is something called a clear conscience. The rikshaw puller might be toiling throughout the day, but when he finishes the work, the satisfaction he derives in wiping the sweat off his face and drinking a jug of cold water is simply too much. He eats whatever is available and lies down. He has the ability to fall asleep in minutes while the rich and famous keep turning and tossing in their beds for hours before they can fall asleep.'

Srikant, who had been quiet all along, finally commented, 'It all depends on what are your priorities in life. You need to define your priorities. Do you want to make money at any cost or do you want to make money only through ethical means? How much risk are you willing to take to earn the money you want? What sacrifices are you ready to make to earn that money?'

All of them were surprised at these pointblank questions from Srikant. The questions were appearing to be relevant and logical. Yet, they were not very comfortable in answering them right away. They needed some time to think. They needed time to first understand what would be their priorities in life. Then they could plan their actions. It was a matter concerning their life . . . it was not a joke.

They were young and their entire life lay ahead of them. The choices they make today were going to affect their future.

It had to be right . . . for there were no retakes in life.

*   *   *

1973

Srikant was slowly getting used to the Delhi climate. His father was transferred to Delhi 3 months back and they all moved to Delhi. After all in a transferable central government job, there is hardly any choice with the employee about his placement. Yet, they were happy that they got a posting in Delhi as against some B grade town like say Ludhiana or Coimbatore.

Being in Delhi gave Srikant a special feeling as he felt powerful somehow. He used to look at the parliament and say to himself, 'This is the place from where they operate the country and manage millions of people. How powerful they must be.'

He also used to admire the power wielded by the elected representatives when the traffic is stopped for them to pass through. He saw hundreds of people waiting at the signal for the politician to pass through, so that their way would be cleared. And then like a tornado, the swooping cavalcade of cars would speed past the signal in few seconds. The poor traffic constable struggled after every such act to restore traffic as it took nearly half an hour to get back to normalcy.

Srikant felt in his mind, 'Is the time of these people really so important, that they make hundreds of others wait on the roads? What are they really doing?'

One day, his friend asked him whether he was free to join him in an agitation planned in his college. He was not a student of any college as he was looking for a job after completing his BA. He thought it was a good idea to pass time. The friend also informed him that he would be given free Tiffin for participating in the rally. That attracted him more than the unknown cause of the agitation.

Srikant went to the college and soon learnt that the agitation was against the increased bus pass fares for students in the city buses. He too joined the crowd in college as it marched across the main roads of Delhi. Many more college students joined the march as it swelled. He enjoyed the Chhole Bhatoore with onion in the evening.

He felt as though he had earned his 'first income' in his life.

*   *   *

1974

Pankaj was working in administration department of a private company after completing his M.Sc. It was a 9 to 6 job which offered very little excitement to him. However, his salary was the main motivator for him to continue with the job. His father had retired last year and the responsibility of his younger sister's education was entirely upon him.

One day, while he was watching a cricket match played between India and Pakistan on TV on a Sunday, his neighbor's son Jayesh came to their house as their TV was under repair. He carried with him a notebook and a textbook to complete his unfinished homework. Pankaj was surprised and wondered how this boy was going to complete his homework sitting in front of a TV, while an exciting one day match between India and Pakistan was in progress.

During the innings break, Jayesh hesitantly asked Pankaj whether he still remembered how to solve problems in Algebra. Pankaj thought for a moment and said, yes. Immediately Jayesh asked him a doubt he had about a particular problem in Algebra.

Pankaj remembered his high school teacher Ram Upadhye, who was an expert in Mathematics. He had left lasting impressions in his student's mind all through his teaching career.

Pankaj started off in Ram sir's style, 'For any problem in Algebra, first study the problem. Write down the given data. Next identify what is required to find out. Then judge what parameter should be taken as 'x'. If you do these steps correctly, 90% of the problem is solved. Rest of the problem can be solved very easily.'

Jayesh looked at Pankaj as if he was reciting some valuable gems. He followed the steps as advised by Pankaj and solved the problem. He did another problem in same method. And then another problem . . . ! He solved the entire chapter with this method.

He had one doubt in Trigonometry. Again, in Ram sir's style, Pankaj said, 'In all problems of Trigonometry, first convert everything into Sin and Cos. The solution will appear itself.'

It did the magic again. He solved all the remaining problems.

Next day, Pankaj was thinking while having lunch in the office, how well he explained the old logics of Mathematics to Jayesh and how easily he understood it. He was surprised at his good teaching abilities. He wondered whether he would be a good teacher as well.

His subject knowledge was anyway good, as he was a very good student while in school. He had missed a seat in Engineering by a narrow margin; otherwise he was a brilliant student all through.

Throughout the day, he experienced a sense of achievement. Later, on much introspection he realized that this 'kick' was due to the successful teaching he had done yesterday.

CHAPTER 3

Vikram had joined a steel company as a management trainee. He was one of the brightest 150 engineers chosen by the company from a national level test followed by group discussion and interview. He was thrilled to work as an engineer in a mega steel plant, which was still in the final phase of construction.

He was finding it very adventurous to wear the company uniform, board the staff bus from township and head for the factory in the morning at 8 am. He was learning many new things every day. He was a metallurgical engineer and was very much interested in knowing how his studies can help him in performing better at the plant.

The food at the staff canteen was good. He appreciated the fact that all his seniors also stood in the same queue at the lunch time and waited for their turn. He would be served a standard meal of rice, Dal, curry, pickle, curd etc.

As the steel plant was still under construction, the project completion activities were going on at a very fast pace. Deadlines were to be met for inauguration of the plant. He heard from his friends that there were plans to invite the Prime minister for inauguration programme. He felt proud to be a part of the large group involved in making the new steel plant in India.

In the evenings, he used to visit the township club where he played table tennis, chess, carom board etc. There was a small library as well, which had a very good collection of books. He was fond of reading books from his childhood.

As the time passed, he was getting in the groove and he was given more and more responsibilities. He started spending more and more time in the plant. So, while his arrival time at the plant was fixed at 8 am, the departure time was never certain and would vary between 8 pm and 10 pm. On some occasions, he would eat maggi noodles of masala flavor and sleep, as the canteen would have closed by the time he finished working.

As the inauguration date approached, Sundays also became working days and he used to go to his apartment in the staff quarters only for sleeping. It had been a while since he chatted with his friends in a relaxed manner in the club.

Sometimes he wondered, 'What am I achieving with all this?' He was seeing that his seniors were also equally taxed if not more than him. They had families and grown up children as well. He instantly felt pity for the families of his seniors working for the last few months in the plant. But he was a bit worried also, thinking whether this ordeal would continue after the plant inauguration and also after his marriage. If it did, then it would not be a very pleasurable situation where he worked in the plant for 12-14 hours a day, while his newlywed bride sat in home waiting for him to return in the late evening.

He dismissed these disturbing thoughts from his mind and concentrated on his work.

*   *   *

After completing his MBA (Marketing) Amit was selected in the campus interview by a FMCG company as marketing executive. The company was having a national presence with reach in every small town and village of India. Obviously, it was a well established organization with strong work ethics and moral values. He was very happy to move around in formal, well pressed clothes around the city to carry out his assignments as Marketing executive.

Soon, he learnt that Marketing was the only field in which a person could have astronomical growth in relatively short period of time. It all depended on how fast he brings results for the company. And the results in this case meant only one word—sales. The more sales orders he brought for the company, the better would be his performance appraisal.

All the products of his company were very well established. Amit realized that it was an advantage to have established products since less marketing was required. The market inertia would keep the product to keep flowing on the shelves. Even without aggressive marketing, the products would be sold. However, the challenge was in retaining the market share in a world of stiff competition. He used to think in lighter moments, that as long as people brush their teeth regularly and they take bath every day, his company would survive and continue to grow.

However, a few months into the marketing field, he realized that it was not an easy job. The competition was catching up very fast and any minor product quality issue or lax distribution network could dip the sales for the month. He was now required to attend the monthly meetings discussing company's performance during the month. And he was rather surprised to see the amount of pressure his line managers were in, to explain the drop in sales and to make commitments for the next quarter. That was the first time he was seeing the other side of the glamorous marketing job.

However, that somehow seemed to motivate him further. He knew that the same senior management guys, who put pressure and criticized the under-achievement of the team, would also lavishly praise them for surpassing the targets.

He imagined the idea of getting praised by the senior management for his achievements and being rewarded handsomely. The thought of getting called on to stage for receiving an award thrilled him. He even fantasized the speech he would give whenever such an occasion would arise. He would thank god, his parents, the company, his boss, colleagues etc. and share the success with them. He also coined few well known motivational phrases to be used on such occasions like 'There is no substitute for hard work' and 'Every target is achievable with proper planning and focused approach'.

He had a burning desire to be an over achiever . . . !

*   *   *

Pankaj's younger sister was getting married. And the entire family was in a state of happiness and excitement. Pankaj's father had searched a very good match for his daughter. He had been visiting several marriage bureaus since last 6 months and registering her details. And finally his search yielded him good results. The boy was from a respectable family working in a state government job as Upper Division Clerk. The traditional thought always considered a government job as the biggest asset, as it assured a monthly pension after retirement.

Pankaj was organizing and planning all the tasks related to the marriage in a systematic manner. The venue had to be booked, the Brahmin had to be fixed, the catering services to be identified and booked, the invitation cards to be printed and distributed. It was almost like a project work from start to finish.

Pankaj sent special invitations to his best friends Srikant, Amit and Vikram. He was excited to meet them after a gap of almost 5-6 years.

Srikant readily accepted the invitation and booked the train tickets to Mumbai. He was looking forward to meeting all his old friends and also enjoying the marriage ceremony. The fact that he was still unemployed helped him to make a quick decision. However, he was feeling bad that he was still unemployed even after 3 years of finishing his degree. He was not sure, how he would react when the subject came up.

Amit was in Mumbai, so he had no problem at all. He just needed to ensure that he organizes his monthly tour in such a way that he will be in Mumbai on the wedding day. These days, Amit was spending almost 23 days in a month in touring his marketing territory extensively.

Vikram was very happy to see the marriage invitation reach him by post. It actually brought tears in his eyes to see a communication from his old friend after such a long time. He was so busy in the plant commissioning works that he had almost forgotten his personal life. He used to talk to his parents once in a fortnight, generally after 11 pm to take the benefit of the low STD rates. He was not sure whether his leave application would be sanctioned, as he had seen his senior colleagues hesitate to approach the manager with their leave applications. Unfortunately, while sanctioning leave, the manager behaved as though the person going on leave was the most important person in the entire organization and in his absence, the commissioning would get indefinitely delayed.

The marriage was performed in the best possible manner that Pankaj's father could afford. Pankaj had taken loan from his company to meet the expenses. In spite of the financial constraints, they did not cut corners anywhere in fulfilling the 'social obligations' like video shooting, the band, the buffet lunch etc.

The day after marriage, Pankaj got some time to sit and relax for the first time in the last several days. He had almost singlehandedly carried out all the preparations for the marriage. The tent in front of the house was removed, chairs were counted and taken away, and the caterer had also vacated the function hall.

Vikram had managed to get two days leave with much difficulty to attend the marriage. He was leaving by the train in the evening. They decided to meet in a nearby park before he left so that they can remember the memories for few more months.

The children were playing in the park all over the grass. Some enthusiastic people were playing shuttle, badminton and tennicoit. The four friends were looking at the park proceedings as if lost in some old thoughts. They were eating roasted salty peanuts in paper cones and enjoying it very much.

Vikram said, 'Pankaj, thanks for inviting me for your sister's marriage. I enjoyed the train journey, I met my parents, I got a chance to meet all you guys . . .'

Srikant said, 'Yes, I am also very happy. See, Delhi atmosphere is very different from that of Mumbai. In Mumbai you feel that you are a part of the crowd, whether you are in a local train or on a platform. But in Delhi, you are always a different person. There is always a feeling of separation between you and the others around you. You can never really mix with the crowd as it happens here.'

Amit said, 'Guys why do you have to be a part of the crowd? Think differently. Whether crowds accept you or not, do not attempt to be a part of the crowd. Create your own entity.'

Everyone sensed the change in the direction of the topic.

Amit continued, 'What matters in the end is what recognition you are able to achieve in the society you live. Nothing else matters.'

Vikram said, 'Amit, why are you so much after getting recognition? Would you be comfortable to live a life where you are given full recognition, but you are required to work for 18 hours a day?'

Amit said instantly, 'Yes, of course. One must struggle to achieve excellence in his life. Even if it means working for long hours, it should be acceptable.'

Vikram thought for a while as if hesitating whether to say something or not. Finally he said, 'Amit, it is very easy to say this but very difficult to practice it. Do you know for instance that I am currently working for 14 hours a day without a weekly break and getting really tired out of it? I seriously feel sometimes that I am burning out myself. I need a time for myself. I need to be alone for sometime everyday to let my creativity take shape. I need to enjoy life like a common man. I want to enjoy TV serials; I want to relax in the evenings . . .'

Suddenly Vikram realized that he was speaking out his innermost feelings suppressed for the past few months now. Apparently, his subconscious mind was waiting for a right audience and an appropriate time to speak out his feelings.

Everyone was looking at Vikram almost in a shock, feeling the pain of his sufferings.

Vikram continued after a while, 'Guys, life is not all about professional achievements and recognition. It is much beyond that. All the guys working in my steel plant are currently getting burnt out day after day. There is no end in sight for their ordeal. Life is passing by us every day. A day gone will never come back in our lives. We should pause for a while every now and then and assess whether we are spending our days the way we wanted to live. If we are not, then we are on a wrong track. We need to correct ourselves. It is never late . . .'

There was a long silence after this outburst from Vikram as though everyone was evaluating in their minds about their respective lives and checking whether they were living a life they wanted to live. No one had a ready answer to say confidently a yes or a no.

They wished one another goodbye as it was getting late for Vikram to catch his train at 10.30 pm. They dispersed thinking in their minds about how their circumstances had changed . . . and with it their ideologies.

CHAPTER 4

One day, while Pankaj was having lunch in the office, he was thinking about his outstanding loan and the means of repaying it. This was the thought going on in his mind ever since the marriage function was over. Because, he did not like the idea that he owed money to a person or an institution.

He casually picked up the newspaper kept in the office canteen and started reading the classified advertisement. Generally classified advertisements are a place in the newspaper where one can find all sorts of business proposals, invites, schemes, ideas etc. His attention was captured by an advertisement for coaching classes. It was an advertisement by a small institute offering coaching classes for various entrance examinations.

He thought for a while. He remembered that he had recently clarified some concepts of Algebra and Trigonometry to Jayesh. He also recollected that Jayesh had learnt it quickly and that he himself had a feeling of satisfaction of having explained it. He wondered whether he can start taking tuitions. Maths was his favorite subject and he had realized recently that he was still good at it.

He immediately typed on a white sheet of paper 'Maths Tuitions for class VIII, IX and X' on an A4 size paper. He was wondering where he shall display this paper. He felt awkward to display it on the front door of his house. Because, once he displays it there, instantly everyone in the chawl would come to know about it. However, after some contemplation, he thought that he had to stick it on his house only because, once he started the tuitions, anyway neighbors would come to know about it.

That night he pasted the paper on his front door and slept. He was wondering what kind of response that would fetch from his neighbors. He almost looked with pride at that paper when he left for the office the next day.

When he returned back in the evening, his mother told him that two of his neighbors had already enquired about the tuitions and the fees. He was very happy to see some response to his efforts and the adventure. He went to his neighbors and told them that he would charge Rs. 25/- per month for each student. The deal was done.

Within one week of starting the tuitions, the word spread around and he had now 17 students. He spent the evenings by taking tuitions. As he was very good in the subject and also he had good communication skills, the students understood the concepts he taught quickly. Gradually he was relieved from the thoughts of how he was going to repay the loans.

But more than the joy of earning additional money, what surprised him was that he was actually enjoying teaching maths to the students.

Soon, Pankaj started enjoying his newly found love for teaching. He used to go to the office in the morning as usual and look forward to the evenings when he would sit with all the children around him listening to him and learning from him. Somehow, the satisfied expressions on the faces of children when they understood the subject pleased him immensely.

Since last month, he had started taking two batches as the space was not enough for accommodating all the children at a time. He separated them class wise. The students of Eighth and Ninth grade were in one batch and those in tenth grade were in a different batch. Both the batches had 25 students each. Anymore addition to the existing capacity would have required him to rent a room somewhere for this purpose.

He was getting occasional enquiries for taking more admissions, but due to lack of space he refused them. He did not want to compromise on the quality of his teaching. Already his efforts were yielding results, as the students were obtaining good marks in their unit tests and the assignments.

His loan amount also was getting repaid at a pace faster than he had imagined. At this rate, he would be free from the loan in next 4 months. The thought of financial freedom pleased him. He would then spend some money for himself and his family. However, he never fancied any expensive luxuries in life. His principle was that one should spend only what one can earn. He would rather save the money in some fixed deposits instead of spending them away on wasteful things.

He had to take care of his younger brother's education as well. He planned to make him study as much as he wanted. He thought of realizing his unfulfilled professional dreams through his brother. His brother was also one of his students in his tuitions. And all other students envied his brother for living in such close proximity to the storehouse of information and knowledge.

The next academic year was about to begin and he started getting enquiries for admission from now itself. He located a good 18 feet by 26 feet room on the first floor of a commercial complex in his locality. The rent was also less. Now he could take more admissions. He started four batches of 50 students each. That gave him an income more than double of what he earned in his full time job during the day.

He soon started contemplating whether he needed to continue with his job at all. Because, he was steadily earning good money from his tuitions and working for 8-10 hours in his job made him somewhat tired to take the four batches. So, after much hesitation, he took the bold step and one day resigned from his company to concentrate fully on the tuitions.

Now, he used to relax during the day and start gearing up for long hauls of 5-6 hours teaching from 4 pm onwards every day.

And he liked it.

*   *   *

Srikant had come to Jantar Mantar to participate in a dharna staged by some social organizations against the price rise. Actually he came to know about that through the newspaper. He sat there among the public, in the front row, facing the temporarily erected dais on which the leaders were sitting. The slogans were being raised continuously from all sides, criticizing the government policies and their inaction in controlling the price rise.

The place was also swarming with media people to cover the event. Suddenly from somewhere one media person appeared in front of him and started asking him questions.

The media person asked him, 'Sir, why are you here?'

Srikant at first hesitated but then answered, 'I am here to protest against the government policies. They are not doing enough to control the prices. How will the poor men survive in such conditions?'

The media person said, 'Sir, what steps you feel the government should take to arrest the price rise?'

Srikant thought for a second and said, 'The government should appoint a committee immediately to review the prices. They should prepare plans on what subsidies can be given to the poor people. They should draw plans to import the food stuff which is in shortage in India. Actually there are many things the government can do. All it needs is a strong will to help the people.'

The media person looked interested in this spirited talk from an unassuming person. The media person was also happy that he was actually recording the conversation which would improve the quality of his coverage of this news item, making his bosses happy. So, he continued the conversation.

He asked, 'Sir, do you mean to say that the government is not doing enough currently to meet the requirements of the people?'

Srikant again started off, 'Yes of course. The government is probably forgetting that they are in power because the common man has voted them into power. They need to listen to the Janata of this country. If they think that they can do anything for 5 years once elected, they are under a very wrong impression. The mightiest of government will crumble under the public pressure, if they deviate from the established norms of governance.'

By then, a small crowd had gathered around them to listen to what appeared to be a very strong message. The leaders from the stage were also curious to know about this person, who was able to arouse the interest from the crowds, by his statements alone.

That day evening, a white ambassador car stopped in front of Srikant's house. A medium built person in a gray safari suit came out and started asking for Srikant. Srikant was reading newspaper inside his house. He was surprised that someone had come looking for him in an ambassador car.

He came out and said he was Srikant. The person in the Safari suit said, 'Namashkar . . . I am Jayant Mehra . . . the Personal assistant of Sukhram ji.'

Srikant was shocked. Sukhram was the MLA of their constituency. With his astonished look he enquired, 'Namashkar . . . how may I help you?'

Jayant replied, 'Sir ji has called you for a meeting. He has seen your 'media briefing' in today's protest at the Jantar Mantar. He wishes to talk to you . . .'

Srikant had mixed feelings in his mind as he sat in the white Ambassador car along with Jayant on the way to Sukhram's house. He wondered whether there was any plan to eliminate him because of his outbursts against the government in the media. But from the way Jayant treated him, it did not appear so. He was being courteous enough which gave some hope that the invitation was in good faith and for good reasons.

The car entered the sprawling bunglow of Sukhram. There were lush green lawns inside the compound. He spotted Sukhram sitting on a chair in the lawn with some people around him. They appeared to be his party workers. The scene was normal and there was no animosity in the air. The tempers were appearing cool.

Jayant led Srikant to Sukhram. Sukhram noticed their arrival and signaled his party workers to leave. Now only the three were present there.

Sukhram looked at the moving leaves of a low hanging branch of a tree nearby for a while and then said, 'So you are Srikant . . . you talk very well.'

Srikant did not know how to respond to that. He did not even know whether it was to be taken as a compliment or a skill that would land him in trouble.

He did not say anything. He kept looking at the centre table, avoiding eye contact with Sukhram.

Sukhram said, 'What do you do?'

Srikant said in a low voice, 'Sir, I am searching for a job as of now. I have completed B.A and currently studying law through correspondence.'

Sukhram said, 'Would you like to work with us?'

Srikant was surprised at this straight invitation from a politician.

He said, 'Sir, what kind of work?'

He then wondered whether it was correct to ask this question, because a politician definitely would not ask him to preach and demonstrate morality to the people.

Sukhram said, 'See Srikant, we are currently strengthening the party. We need young people who have good communication skills and who have some rational ideas. This is our essential requirement as we need to propagate our policies to the young masses in next three years.'

Srikant was happy. He already started visualizing his role in the party.

Seeing his expression, Jayant intervened, 'So can you join us, Srikant?'

Srikant thought for a while about asking for the remuneration details. But he did not think it appropriate to ask.

He just nodded his head. Jayant asked the driver to drop Srikant at his house.

On the way back, Srikant was seeing the world in a totally different perspective . . . through the window of an ambassador car.

And it looked very nice indeed.

*   *   *

Amit had now become the regional manager of the company he started working with just 4 years ago. He had been a star performer all through this period and that fetched him multiple promotions apart from handsome salary increments and generous bonus from the company. His influence in the company was growing by the day.

The general manager took him to all important policy meetings concerning the Product launch strategies, Business growth strategies, New Product development strategies etc.

Amit was also given a new car by the company in line with company's policy. He took much pride in moving around the roads of Mumbai n the car. Whenever he went past the school in which he studied, he used to look at it and think of his childhood days. Sometimes he used to feel how good those days were, when the only tension in life was about doing the homework and preparing for exams. There were no sales targets, no worries about market competition, no busy schedules, no meetings with clients etc.

Amit used to travel for 27 days in a month. He was made in-charge for the south and west zone markets in India. That meant he travelled to all the major cities in South and West India like Madras, Bangalore, Hyderabad, Cochin, Trivandrum, Ahmadabad, Goa, Jaipur etc. It was a big area and required his attention and focus all the time. His work was only to hold meetings in these cities, evaluate the performance of his teams, do the fish-bone analysis for the problems, find out solutions, define and fix the targets for the next month/Quarter etc.

He had all the luxuries while on travel. Like second class AC travel, accommodation in three star hotels, taxi booked in all the cities throughout his stay, all bills paid by the company with no questions asked. The company also trusted him, as he was bringing business and making money for the company. Some statistics suggested that the company's growth was fuelled by the growth in the region controlled by him as it was significantly contributing to the national growth figures.

One day, while Amit was sitting in his office planning for next week's trip to Ahmadabad and Baroda, he was called by his manager. He went there and was surprised to see his National director sitting in his office. They both were discussing something when he entered the cabin and stood up as soon as they saw him.

They handed him a letter stating that he has been promoted as Head of Marketing at the National level. He was pleasantly surprised. This was totally unexpected for him. He knew that he had been a good performer in the company. But a national role was something big . . . really big. He thanked them with gratitude and said," Sir, I shall do my best to live up to your expectations. I know that you are giving me a huge responsibility and that I may have to really work hard to get the expected results. However, I shall try not to let you down in your faith and belief in my capabilities."

He walked back to his cabin with thrill and excitement. He looked at the large India map hung on the wall of the cabin . . . moving his eyes from Kashmir to Kanyakumari and from Ahmadabad to Kolkata. He had seen the map many times before, but it had acquired a new meaning for him today. It was going to be his new Karma bhoomi for the next few months . . . !

*   *   *

The steel plant was commissioned with much fanfare and the inauguration ceremony went off very well. As scheduled, the Prime minister had come for the opening ceremony of the plant. Vikram was very happy to be part of the function. He felt as though his efforts for all these months had borne fruits.

After the inauguration, the plant started its operations. Just like every new plant, this plant also had many teething issues. Every day, there used to be some problem or other which kept the entire operations and maintenance teams in the plant on their toes for long hours. It almost became a 16 hours a day job for Vikram.

One day, due to severe exhaustion, he fell ill. He was taken to the township's doctor, who diagnosed him to be suffering from extreme fatigue and advised him bed rest for at least two weeks to recuperate. Vikram was admitted to the hospital for the first time in his life. He had rarely visited a doctor in his life all these years and now, the circumstances demanded that he spent few days in the hospital. However, he also realized that he was getting too stressed and did not resist getting admitted into the hospital.

For first few hours, he was relaxed, lying in the bed and thinking of all things that mattered to him. He felt as though it was a sort of blessing in disguise that he was out of action for some time. In fact, he even enjoyed closing his eyes for few minutes and lying still. In the past few months, whenever he rested on his bed in his apartment, he fell asleep within few moments due to extreme tiredness. So, it was almost like a luxury for him to be fully awake, yet close his eyes and think of something in his mind.

On the second day in the hospital, he started missing the plant. He felt that the world was racing ahead and he was lying still in one corner. He wanted to be in action. He was missing it very badly. He started just walking slowly around his bed to feel the action. He was thinking about his colleagues and what they would be doing right now. How they got up early in the morning, rushed to catch the company bus which took them from the township to the plant, how they must have had their breakfast in the company canteen within 3-4 minutes in order to be on time, how they must have worn their helmets and walked into the plant area . . .

Today he was not among them because of a problem. However, the plant operations did not stop for him. That made him slightly sad. It meant that while the plant had occupied his life fully, the plant had nothing to do with his well being. For that matter, if any of those hundreds working in the plant had a similar issue, the plant would not have stopped working. It was not that he wanted to have more importance in the plant, yet the fact that it had no slightest effect without him made him unhappy.

Suddenly he thought that he wanted to be away from this entire environment. He was not feeling any more comfortable. He felt as though he was wasting his precious time there. He thought that he was getting burnt out when he should be actually enjoying his life. He wondered why he should not be leading a comfortable life. Why should he be always under stress and strain? Why he cannot relax for a few moments every day? Why?

With these thoughts he slept off. He dreamt that night that he was walking in a garden lined with flowery bushes on both sides. There was a cool breeze which made the walk more pleasant. There was a kind of freshness in the air. The tender rays of the morning sun were falling over him and his body felt the gentle warmth of the sunrays. His mind was in a very happy and relaxed state . . .

Yet, it was only a dream.

CHAPTER 5

Amit was in the new role now for almost six months and had already proved his worth to the company. He had doubled the overall sales of the company during this period. Some of the territories had registered even 300% growth compared to previous years. The management was very happy with him.

One day while going through the company's balance sheet and the profit and Loss account for last year, he observed that the company had made Rs. 30 Crore profit. He knew that his contribution was most significant in this achievement. That means the company had made a profit of Rs. 30 Crores and paid him only a few Lakhs in return. Somehow it did not appeal to him that he makes all the efforts for the company and the company retains most of the profits, while giving him smaller amounts.

He wanted to get the entire profits. He was not going to be satisfied with what the company paid him as salary and allowances. He started feeling as though the company had not been treating him fairly all these years.

He sat in his office looking through the window outside. He saw the road and the traffic outside. Few years back he used to walk on these roads to the school. Then he started moving on a scooter, and then a company owned Mercedes Benz car.

Now he wanted to raise the bar. He wanted to own a company. He started saying to himself . . . Be the boss of yourself. No one will give you targets. No need to say 'sir' to anyone. Come to the office whenever you want. No need to apply for leave at all. The company runs on your directions. You decide what is to be done and what is not to be done. You make policies for the company.

This thought distracted him very much from his work. He could not concentrate on the files he was looking at. Actually he was preparing for an important meeting scheduled for next week. But nothing was going into his head, as the highway of his thought process was jammed with the idea of becoming a master of his own destiny.

He wondered what obstacles he would face in starting his own business. What risks would he take in switching over the role from a senior manager of an established company to that of an owner of a new company? As far as the time was concerned, now also he was devoting his full time for the company. So, there would not be a big difference in that aspect. If the question about taking more responsibility was there, he was doing that now too. He did a thorough SWOT analysis of his new idea.

He was convincing himself in his mind to take plunge and start his own business. He wanted to be the boss . . . he wanted to give interviews to the business magazines about how he climbed the ladder of success. He wanted to describe what prompted him to start his own venture. He wanted to be in the limelight beyond his company. Currently, only the people in his company knew him . . . he wanted to be known outside his company as a flamboyant businessman.

More than money, it was the fame and power that attracted him more and more to take the plunge . . . !

After much deliberation, Amit quit the job to start his own business. Being in various responsible positions in the industry for quite some time, he was well aware of the intricacies of the business.

He started his business by taking the distributorship of his company products first. He was well aware of the entire distribution network in the country up to the district level. That helped him significantly in getting on with the business immediately. Very soon he controlled the national distribution of the company products.

Then he went on to expand his area of operation into other non-competing products manufactured by other companies. He acquired the distribution rights of another 6 companies within the next few months and had his presence in every major city by way of some product or other. His investment had already paid off and now he was in the profit making zone. Being only in the distribution field, he had no issues associated typically with manufacturing facilities like raw material supplies, quality control of products, labor unrest etc.

One day while he was shopping in a super market, he got an idea. Why shouldn't he diversify into the super market segment of business? The price increases for any FMCG product by almost 40-60% by the time it leaves factory and reaches the retail customer. By taking the distributorship and dealership of various products, he was earning a good percentage of this profit margin on various products. Now, there was an opportunity to extend his gains and earn the last component of profit by entering retail segment by opening super markets. He was excited with the idea.

After getting a thorough research by consultants, he zeroed in on a location and size for the first mega market in Mumbai. It was the first of a kind where one can get everything under one roof. It had different sections for groceries, stationery, electronics, clothes, plastics and steel, cosmetics etc. There were different sections within the super market for special regional products catering to the population of that region settled in Mumbai. For example, there was a section for products from Calcutta, Madras, Ahmadabad, Ludhiana, Cochin etc. The people from these places flocked in those sections for special products available only in those places.

Amit had always considered that customer service played a major role in every business. Unless the customer is satisfied, a business cannot flourish, however great the quality or price may be. That is why he trained each and every member of his staff on customer care matters. Whenever any of his staff came across a customer inside the super market, they would wish them by having an eye contact and a pleasant smile. Also, he had appointed some staff at strategic locations only to help the undecided customers or confused customers about any product location within the super market. That ensured that every customer walking in his super market had a special feeling of being taken care of.

Amit gave lot of importance to the ambience. According to him, if the ambience is good, people feel encouraged to spend more and left them highly satisfied. So, he put bright lights inside the alleys and also played music in low volume all the time. The hit songs of new released films were being played so that people also get the thrill of listening to their favorite music while shopping. And finally, there were toffees and chocolates kept at the counter which were given free of cost to the children accompanying their parents. The trick was that children would be happy to get these unexpected gifts and every parent will become happy to see his child happy as well.

The super market was a big hit and did brisk business from day one. It started making profits much before he anticipated. That gave birth to his idea of expanding the supermarkets to other cities. Soon, he had supermarkets in 16 major cities of India. That helped him further in negotiating attractive deals with various suppliers. Moreover, the transport arrangements were made more efficient by way of using the transport carriers at discounted rates while returning from a place, filled with goods from that place.

Amit believed the key to success in any business lay only in two things. The first was customer satisfaction and second was quality of service. That is why he created some very good customer feedback systems since he believed that no business can survive or grow unless it listens to its customers. The customer needs are very dynamic in nature and keep changing continuously. The businesses which adapted quickly to customer requirements had fair chances of growth. He appointed a senior level manager to look after all the customer complaints and suggestions. Sometimes he used to personally read the complaints made by customers.

One day he read a complaint from a customer about a defective pack of washing powder. The customer complained that the pack was not sealed properly and quantity was also less. The pack was exchanged immediately by the staff, as per management policy and the defective pack was retained for defect analysis. Amit somehow felt that he should look at the defective pack. He asked for the defective pack and it was brought to his office by the office boy. Amit realized at one glance that it was a duplicate pack. He was shocked. He always took pride in the fact that his outlets always sold the original products. So, he was worried as to from where this duplicate pack came into his stores?

His further enquiries revealed that the purchase manager had actually bought the duplicate product at the cost of original product and taken some commission in the process. Amit was enraged. He immediately ordered removal of all the stock of that product from the shelves and also fired the purchase manager immediately. He did not show leniency toward someone who broke his trust. He did not mind non-performance of a person because the performance can always be improved by proper training or by empowerment to take necessary decisions and sometimes a proper work environment. But he never tolerated the wrong attitude of any staff. He felt that attitude is something which is very hard to change and almost impossible in many cases. Similarly, he valued the integrity of a person. Integrity is something which would ensure that the person always kept the company's interests above his personal interests. One act of dishonesty was enough for the person to get the lure of personal gains and it soon becomes a habit. With every act of corruption, the person becomes emboldened to do more, because the human needs are infinite and they cannot always be met with official and legitimate means. That is why Amit always believed in nipping in the bud, any acts of misuse of power for personal gains, by any of his staff. Such acts, apart from acting against the interest of the company, also endangered its reputation. According to him, it takes years to build a reputation for the company but it takes only one incident to lose it. And once a reputation is lost, it takes lot of effort and time to rebuild it all over again.

His next big venture was to expand beyond India. He started off with distributorships and dealerships in African countries like Kenya, Tanzania, Zimbabwe, and Nigeria etc. He often visited those countries to oversee the operations. He had appointed a proper hierarchy in every country so that accountability was properly defined and responsibilities assigned. Many times during this expansion process beyond the country, he came across several instances when he was offered the route by which he could subvert the laws of that land to save some of his set-up costs. However, he always believed in business ethics and respected every government. He did not want to be ever caught on the wrong side of the law by any agency. That ensured his peace of mind.

Then he moved to the Far East countries like Malaysia, Thailand and Hong Kong. Very soon, he was having a business running in more than 23 countries around the world with a business turnover of more than US $ 5 Billion and a combined workforce of 3,000 people.

One thing which Amit took special care of while expanding his business was that he never violated any laws. He believed in doing business ethically by following all the rules of land. That way, he never had any problems worrying about the enforcement agencies. He had advised his finance director that he did not want to evade a single paisa tax to the local government. He always complied with all the statutory requirements.

He had become a business tycoon. His name started appearing in the various business forums and his story was covered in almost all standard business journals. He also won the coveted 'fastest upcoming entrepreneur' award by the prestigious British chamber of commerce and Industry.

At 36, he was one of the youngest Billionaires in the world.

*   *   *

Vikram had spent already one week in the hospital and was experiencing a new kind of freedom . . . it was the freedom from the hard daily routine of his factory life. He used to get up late in the morning without thinking about catching the company bus or punching his attendance in time at the security main gate. He did not worry about what problems existed in the plant yesterday night, something which he did every day while walking in the plant every morning. He did not have to think of the daily production figures. If the figures were good, the operations department took credit for that and if they were not, then maintenance team would be blamed for some breakdowns resulting in the shortage of these figures.

He was not averse to working hard, but he was not comfortable with working hard every day without an end in sight. That amounted to wasting one's life, according to him. A person needs to lead a balanced life to be happy. He needs to divide his time on work and family in a fair ratio, so as not to hurt any sphere of the life. Too much of work would have spoiled his family life and too much of attention and involvement with family meant less career growth. Both the extremes were not looking very attractive. He had read somewhere that a person is really in control of his life, when he has both the money and time to do the things he desires. For example, there are many people in this world who like to go on expensive vacations, but they cannot as they have no money. And then there are equal number of people who can afford to go on expensive vacations, but they do not have the time. They do not get leave from the company.

Vikram wanted to define the optimum balance between the different spheres to lead a satisfied life. He felt that this information would enable thousands of people to enjoy this beautiful life. But how was he going to define it unless he has enough knowledge about it? He needed to study it first before understanding it and advising others. He enquired from the nurse whether there was any library in the hospital. She said, "Yes, there is one good library with a storehouse of new books on various subjects. He wanted to see if there are any books dealing in solving this biggest human mystery about the optimum work and personal life balance in a person's life. He consulted the librarian and went to the 'self help' books section. There he found books written by many authors like Wayne Dyer, Deepak Chopra, Zig Zagler, Jim Rohn, Les Brown, Mark Victor Hansen, Dan Millman, Jack Canfield, Stephen Covey and Dale Carnegie etc.

He picked up one of the books and started reading it . . . he found it very interesting.

*   *   *

Pankaj was now fully settled in his new set up. He had earned a name for himself in the coaching classes industry. He had rented a new place for his coaching classes. There were 5 rooms in his new coaching centre. He had also hired some very good teachers for sharing his load. He knew that the quality of teaching was paramount to the success of any coaching centre, so he personally interviewed every applicant. He always looked for passion in the person whom he selected.

All his loans were repaid now and he had started buying some luxury items for his house. He had nourished a dream of owning a music system, a guitar and a good collection of books. He got them all, thanks to the good amount of money he was now earning from the coaching classes. However, he never seemed to be greedy for money. He welcomed the windfall of money but he never blindly followed money. He knew that money comes and goes. What remains are the values of a person and his image in the society he lives in.

During his leisure time in the afternoon, he started reading ancient scriptures like Bhagwad Gita and Upanishads. He was a religious minded person from the beginning and so he wanted to read these books for a very long time, but never found the leisure time before. The more he read these books, the more interest he developed in them. He read various editions of these books by eminent authors and started understanding the deeper meaning of life.

He started thinking of where we come from and where we go from here. What is the real purpose of our life on earth? What counts as 'Punya' and what is considered as 'Paapa' in the final tally in Chitragupta's durbar? These thoughts started occupying his mind like never before.

And one day he realized that life of a human being was meant to worship God of course, but along with that it was meant to help others in need. He strongly started believing that his knowledge, money and time must be utilized for the benefit of others who are in need of it.

He started wondering whether he was following the righteous path right now. He was teaching the students maths and collecting remuneration in return. He wondered whether he had converted the noble act of disseminating knowledge into a commercial transaction. Was he selling the knowledge? He knew that knowledge was nobody's prerogative and everyone interested and ready to put in hard work can acquire it. Then how come he is collecting any remuneration for that?

These thoughts disturbed him. He started feeling guilty about the entire concept of collecting fees for the coaching classes. He felt that by collecting the fees, he was helping himself. He was not helping the students. If he really wanted to help others, then he should not collect any fees. Moreover, he should teach those who need the assistance in learning but cannot bear the cost of learning in today's world.

Yes . . . this idea appealed to him very much. He should be teaching the students who are capable of learning, yet do not have the necessary resources to learn. And he should not collect any money towards this. That would be termed as the real contribution to the society.

That day, for the first time ever since he had started the coaching classes, he did not enjoy teaching, as he felt that he was selling education, which did not have concurrence of his sub-conscious mind.

Pankaj sat one day with his wife and seriously discussed about his thought process. He said to her that he did not enjoy the 'teaching for a cost' anymore. He said, it was a sin to sell knowledge and education. If he possessed some knowledge, it was his prime duty to pass it on to others and any charges for that was unethical.

They both discussed the issue for long hours and finally decided to quit the coaching classes business. They had made enough money by then, to survive for rest of their lives. So, money was not at all a criterion. Usually, all human endeavors, creativity and courage get stunted when there is no financial freedom. Many people in this world cannot pursue higher objectives because they do not have money to survive for more than 3-4 months without their monthly salaries. This fact binds them to continue their jobs and carry on with the routine year after year till their retirement.

Pankaj calculated the risks of not earning for the rest of his life. Would he be able to survive? Would he be able to meet the aspirations of his family members? Would he afford to live a comfortable life? Would he be able to provide a decent education to his son? How would the society react to him?

Finally Pankaj decided to shift to his father's village, Shantinagar which was some 300 km from Mumbai. It was a small town with minimal infrastructure like roads and proper sanitation facilities. He wanted to open a school there and provide free education for children who cannot afford to go to cities. That way, he would repay to the society what he received from the almighty. The power of Knowledge . . . !

He visited Shantinagar with his family and spoke to the village sarpanch about opening a school there. The people of Shantinagar were very happy to know about this proposal. They were very happy that their children could now learn to read and write and carve a better future for themselves.

They were almost seeing God in Pankaj. They had heard that God does not appear in the form in which we worship him. He chooses to appear in the form of one among us at appropriate time. However, often we fail to recognize and understand his blessings. Many times he does not grant us what we earnestly desire for our own benefit in future. But the human mind is too small to decipher the blessings and get carried away in emotions of not getting what it wanted.

On Ugadi day, Pankaj started off his school. He and his wife would teach all the children in Shantinagar. There were only two classes, one for boys and one for girls. They were first taught ABCD and then 123 and then words and sentences.

Pankaj's aim was very clear. He just wanted to put them on rails and push them. Thereafter, they would have to acquire their own energy to run faster. So, he used to teach them the basics and a lot of moral values. After that they would have to go to the nearby towns and cities to learn further. He was satisfied that he was creating a better future for many children in Shantinagar, who would have otherwise grown up to become laborers in agricultural fields or doing some menial jobs.

He did not collect any money from anyone for this school. He named the school 'Vidya Vardhini'. He also gave scholarships to the brilliant students so that they get encouraged to achieve further excellence in their academics in future.

*   *   *

Srikant's biggest asset was his gift of gab. He had the ability to talk and convince people with his viewpoint. He had no stage fear. Therefore, Srikant was made the secretary of the youth wing and sent to various colleges to mobilize the students in participating in various rallies organized by the Jansatta Party. And he had been fairly successful in galvanizing the support of the students. Many political parties need the support of students to survive and grow. In the process, many careers get destroyed because many students really do not have the maturity of thought to understand what is right and what is wrong for them, at this crucial phase in their lives.

Srikant was now one of the promising young leaders of his party and he was in the forefront in every function organized in the region. On all the posters and hoardings of Jansatta Party, the size of his photo had increased significantly from being a small face among many, in a corner somewhere, to just a bit smaller than the national and regional leaders of the party.

It was after nearly three years of his meeting Sukhram that he was nominated for the position of Municipal corporater of his area. Getting a ticket was not easy, as there were too many contenders for the position. He was sure that Sukhram played a key role in recommending his name to the high command. He won the elections by an impressive margin and was very happy.

He had an office of power now. His signatures were a lot more important than they were before. Without his signatures, many things in his area of jurisdiction would come to a standstill. People would come to him with proposals and application forms for obtaining approvals. He enjoyed the idea that people would queue up in front of his office waiting for their turn to meet him. An office boy in white uniform would handle the flow of people in his office.

As he started working, he got to know many things about which he had no idea before. For example, a new theatre was to be constructed in his area. The theatre owner came to him to get his approval before obtaining any other approvals like electricity or water supply. His secretary told him that registration of every single business activity in his area needed his approval.

It was a memorable day for Srikant when he gave approval for the first time to an ice cream factory. The owner had come to his office the next day and gave him a small packet.

He asked, 'What is this?'

The person replied with a big smile on his fat face, 'Sir, this is a small gift from our side.'

Srikant quickly understood that it contained money. He said, 'But I did not ask for this . . .'

The person, with an even bigger smile, said, 'Sir, that is your greatness. But this is out of our happiness. Please accept it for our sake.'

Srikant just looked at him and said, 'Ok, fine. Thanks.'

And he secretly opened the packet after the person left his office. It contained Twenty Thousand rupees. That was a big money for him. He had not seen this much amount earlier.

Thereafter, it became almost a routine for him to receive such amounts from various applicants. He started living a life of luxury. He purchased a spacious 2 bedroom apartment in a suburban area. He bought jewellary and started wearing a gold chain and three rings on his fingers.

He became popular among the business community in his area for helping them with his prompt approvals without creating much fuss. Sometimes, he even gave approvals at lesser costs, when the person requested him for discounts.

Slowly Srikant started dreaming of even bigger powers. He wanted to become a MLA, since a MLA had many more powers than a municipal corporater.

And one day when the state elections were round the corner, he approached Sukhram, his mentor to put his request—for playing a larger role in politics.

In the next 6 years, by his 'hard work', Srikant became the MP of his party. He was in politics now for a long time and learnt all the tricks required for being in the limelight all the time. He was not very honest, but not outright dishonest either. He made money wherever possible and whenever it came by itself, but never demanded money or rejected any proposals because he got less money than he expected from the deal.

His name started appearing in local newspapers and every move of his was being covered by the media wherever he went and whichever function he attended. He was very cautious in his media briefings as he knew very well that the media was news hungry and had immense potential as well as desire to twist the news to make it appear sensational for the masses.

His stature grew to the extent that he had the contact numbers of high profile people like Collector, Mayor and the Police Commissioner. There used to be a tight security for him wherever he went. He knew that the police force did not have real respect for politicians from their heart, yet they were bound by their duty to provide security. Behind their stoic faces, he could sense their feelings of anguish and hatred as well. However, like every other politician, he went around with a smiling face as though he was oblivious of their true feelings.

Once Sukhram called Srikant to his office and said, 'Srikant, the assembly elections for four states are going to be held early next year. So, we need to start preparing for that.'

Srikant was happy at the thought of helping the party for elections in other states as well, because it meant that his stature at the national level would rise automatically.

Srikant said, 'Yes sir, of course. Give me the command and it would be done.'

Sukhram always appreciated Srikant's positive attitude. He never said no to anything. However difficult the task may be, Srikant thought from various angles, often thinking 'out of the box' and gave some good solutions to the problem. Srikant also had maintained friendly relations with many other party leaders, which kept him informally aware of the other party's views on all the general issues. This was a unique quality, which endeared him to many leaders from across the party lines. Sukhram never regretted for identifying this diamond and nurturing it to higher levels.

Sukhram said, 'Srikant, as an integral part of the preparations for the elections, we need to collect funds for meeting the election expenses like organizing the rallies, distributing money among the rural voters, buying liquor for the lower class voters, buying votes from influential religious and social leaders who have some mass followers etc.'

For the first time Srikant was realizing the exact nature of expense involved in elections. He was not exactly surprised, but felt enlightened. After spending a few years in politics, he came to know many dark truths and realities of politics which are known only to the politicians of the country and which are hidden from the entire population of the country. Some of these things came out occasionally in biographies of the retired politicians, who 'revealed' other's acts of corruption. Many of those accused would have either died by then or become inconsequential for their acceptance or denial of those accusations.

Srikant said, 'Yes sir. But who would give us funds for these expenses?' Are there any specific sources of these funds?'

Sukhram said, 'Contact all the big industrial houses. They give us generous donations from time to time.'

Srikant was surprised. He said, 'But what interest do they have in our party's prospects? How does it affect their business? Why would they part with their hard earned money for our sake?'

Sukhram said as if revealing one more political secret, 'There are several reasons why they donate money to us. First of all, the money donated to political parties is exempted from taxes. However, that is not their main motivator. They get all the approvals for their business expansions faster when they donate funds to us. We process and sanction all their proposals without any delays which benefit their business. However, this is also not their main motivator.'

Srikant was learning something new. He was wondering what the other motivator could be than what he had already heard from Sukhram.

Sukhram continued, 'Their main motivator to donate funds to our party is that during the state and centre budget we take care of them. We reduce the duties and taxes for the products of their company which benefits them in a huge way. And in some cases, we also increase the duties and taxes for the products of their competitors, which again indirectly helps them.'

Srikant was numb. He had never imagined that the business houses could be benefitted from political parties in this manner.

Sukhram concluded, 'Therefore, if we are generating additional profits for them through legal means, they will not have any qualms in giving away a part of it as donations for our cause.'

Srikant went around with his task of contacting the big business houses known to him.

In due course of time, on advice from Sukhram, he had opened an account in Swiss bank to deposit the excess 'unaccounted' money. He also purchased property in three states, many of them in benami accounts or in the name of his driver, maid and gardener. He had also purchased stakes in some industries and was actively involved in the board meetings. There was hardly any luxury in this world which he could not afford to buy.

He had become a successful politician.

CHAPTER 6

Vikram had read just a few books on motivation and self help and his attitude had completely changed. He felt that his life was incomplete the way it was going on currently. There was no fun in working in a factory located in a remote village, day after day for long hours. By doing this, at his retirement he would at best have purchased a house, educated his children and married them off. But that was not life. Life was meant to be much more than that.

He wanted to enlighten the millions of people around the world on the true meaning of life. He wanted to spread the message of the real purpose of life and how best to enjoy it. He wanted people to wake up from their slumber of ignorance and work on a mid-course correction to ensure that at least their balance part of life is spent well.

One could not change the beginning, but by changing the present, one can always have a different and better ending.

Life comprised of nothing but years, months and days. The days built the months and the months built the years. Life was to be lived each moment. It was to be rejoiced with confidence and pleasure and not with fear and disdain. He seemed to have understood the real purpose of life.

In the next few weeks, he read many philosophical books too to understand the real purpose of life. He read Bhagwad Gita, Quran and Bible. He learnt that every scripture actually preached the same things but in different words. He was now equipped with a unique combination of both Spiritual and Management knowledge. And he found too many similarities between the two. In fact, he observed that many modern management philosophies have been already narrated in some ancient text or the other.

He wanted to now spread the message to masses to live life in its true sense. At the end, it was not how many days one lived; it was about how one lived his life. The quantity was not a matter, it was quality. He decided to resign from his job and devote his time completely on delivering lectures in management philosophy. It was a tough decision. All his colleagues were shocked to hear that he planned to resign from his job and spend his entire time in enlightening people about how to live their lives. Some of them thought that he was crazy. It was unthinkable that an engineer working in such a prestigious steel plant would leave his job for such an un-remunerative and listless pursuit.

His parents were also very much against his idea. They worried about his future. They wondered whether any marriage alliance would come for him, as they were actively thinking about getting him married. Finally, Vikram was persuaded to keep the idea pending till he got married and then he was free to do anything he desired. His parent's idea was that once he had responsibility on his shoulders he would automatically think appropriately. Moreover, a wife can influence a person more effectively in taking a joint decision affecting their family.

One fine day Vikram was married to Vineetha, daughter of a colleague of Vikram's father. However, Vikram started explaining to Vineetha his larger interests and how he hated the workplace. She realized that the way they were living they would never be happy, because Vikram did not enjoy his work. She also shared this opinion that one must follow his inner voice and do what pleases him.

After much thought, he left his job in the steel plant to start his own small company called 'True life . . . '. He was very excited to start the venture he had been longing to for such a long time. He had a small office with one receptionist cum typist cum secretary cum office boy. He had a landline phone connection, a fax machine and a type writer. He advertised in local news papers saying that by attending his training programmes people can increase their productivity. He also sent introduction letters to corporate houses and all industries around Mumbai. He started getting some responses and soon the word of mouth publicity worked for him. Everyone who attended the program was all praise for the study material and the way it was presented. Vikram was thoroughly enjoying life . . . after so many years of hardship.

He was now giving lectures around various forums on how to lead a life effectively and efficiently. How to celebrate small successes in life? How to enjoy smaller moments in life? How one can avoid wasting time by waiting for something big to happen? How to improve one's own performance at work, in spending quality time with one's family and maintaining good relations?

He soon became an icon who delivered lectures on management principles with relevant interesting stories and anecdotes from Mythology. People looked forward to listen to him. He became busy to the extent that people were required to take his appointment at least three months in advance.

His popularity spread across India and he started getting invites from different states. He was spending one third of his time on airports and waiting lounges. He became a sort of celebrity. People were thrilled to meet him and hear his words of wisdom.

He became the Management Guru of modern times . . . !

*   *   *

Once, Amit got a business proposal to start a new manufacturing unit in Gurgaon. It was a factory to be set up with an investment of Rs. 43 Crores and set up over an area of 6 acres. The plot size was 20 acres. He was excited about this project, as it would boost his overall profits by significant levels. He advised his Chief Operating Officer, Sundara Rajan to proceed with all the documentation required for the project.

After a week or so, Sundara Rajan came back and informed him that the proposal was facing a hurdle from the government authorities. They were not giving approvals as the proposed factory was violating the environmental norms of the region.

Amit asked Sundara Rajan, 'What is this all about? Why are we not getting approvals? As I understand, our consultants have designed the plant based on latest technology ensuring that all the environmental requirements are met with.'

The COO replied, 'Yes sir, I have investigated this matter. Apparently, the environmental department is not satisfied with our proposal. They are demanding several changes in our design to make it compliant with the current statutory norms. These changes, if effected, would mean that the project needs to be redesigned, the project cost will overrun by around 25% and more importantly, the plant commissioning gets delayed by at least 4-6 months.'

Amit was worried. He did not really understand the whole thing. If something was designed properly, it meant it was correct. Then where is the question of redesigning? And why?

He asked his secretary to send the PRO to him with the complete file.

The PRO, Jayaraj, was a trusted employee of Amit and was an elderly man performing his duties judiciously. His job was one of the dirtiest jobs, since it involved bribing people at every stage. He used his wisdom to identify the powerful people in each government department and the second level people who would take him to those powerful people. And it all cost money.

Jayaraj came to Amit's cabin with little idea that the meeting was going to be to discuss the delays in government approvals for the upcoming project. He carried with him two box files full of relevant correspondence with the various government agencies on this project.

Amit asked him, 'Jayaraj, what is the problem with the government approvals?'

Jayaraj cleared his throat and said hesitatingly, 'Sir, a new minister is heading the environmental division. I suspect that he is the one stopping our approval.'

Amit said, 'But we paid them their regular amounts, right?'

Jayaraj said, 'Yes, sir, we paid the official fees and also the Rs. 10 Lakhs, which is the standard amount for such projects. However, I think they want more. I heard from others also that recently they have increased their rates for approvals.'

Amit asked, 'How much more they want?'

Jayaraj replied, 'I am not very sure. Double, I suppose . . .'

Amit thought for a while. In normal circumstances, he would have said, 'OK please give it off and proceed with the work.' However, he thought of knowing the reasons for this increase.

He said, 'Let us meet the officials. I want to talk to them.'

Jayaraj realized that he wanted to meet the officials not because he did not trust his capabilities in fixing the price or negotiation skills, but to go to the root of the problem. At this rate, the profitability of business would erode away and the not-so-rich entrepreneurs would be discouraged to start any business.

A meeting was fixed by Jayaraj with the pollution officer to discuss this matter.

On the day of the meeting, Amit went along with Jayaraj to meet the pollution officer, who was apparently demanding more money. The posh Cadillac car pulled up in front of the unkempt government office where the pollution officer sat.

Amit went in along with Jayaraj. The pollution officer quickly understood that there is some problem and asked the people sitting in front of him to meet him next week. He also asked the office boy to bring special tea for the guests.

After settling down, the pollution officer asked Jayaraj, 'Oh sir, why did you take all the trouble to come here?

You should have sent a word and I would have come to meet you . . .'

Jayaraj said, smilingly, 'No sir, we need to come to you. The need is ours . . . .'

Amit looked at the officer and asked him, 'What is the problem with our proposal? Why are you delaying it?'

The officer realized that the situation was serious. He said, 'Sir, shall we go out somewhere for lunch? Anyway it is lunchtime and I am hungry . . .'

Amit realized that he was avoiding talking about the money matters in his office. They went to the nearby restaurant for a business lunch.

After ordering a good array of items from the menu card, the officer started speaking.

He said, 'Sir, I know that you do not want to pay more money to get the approvals. But what can we do? The prices have gone up. The new minister is demanding more money for every approval. What can we do?'

Amit and Jayaraj were a little surprised at this revelation. Looking at the eyes of the officer, they knew that he was telling the truth.

Amit asked him, 'And who is this new minister asking for more money?'

The officer replied, 'Srikant Joglekar . . . !'

*   *   *

Pankaj was leading a very happy life in Shantinagar. Having lived in the congested city of Mumbai, he was very happy to live in the natural surroundings with very few double story buildings in it. The freshness in the air could be sensed throughout the day. It was a very natural kind of life with no pollution or contamination in food and water.

His typical day would start before sunrise. He believed that any person getting up in the morning after sunrise was a lazy person. After his daily ablutions, he would do Yoga for a good one hour. This involved physical exercises like Surya Namashkar and various asanas and also breathing exercises like Kapal Bhanti and Anulom Vilom Pranayam. According to him, Surya Namaskar can do to the body what months of dieting cannot and it can do to the mind what no spiritual discourse can. He believed that Kapal Bhanti and Anulom Vilom Pranayam were very useful in maintaining a good health by increasing the oxygen flow to the entire body and proper blood circulation among all vital organs of the body. Many diseases can be cured by regularly practicing these two breathing asanas every day for just half an hour.

After that, he would have a glass of warm water with lemon and honey. That kept his digestive system clear and healthy by flushing out all toxins and unwanted remnants in the body. Many diseases are actually caused due to accumulation of waste toxins inside the body. A regular cleansing of the digestive system also increases the metabolism rate in the body and helps in reducing the weight. Anything that reduces weight is useful for the body since most of the ailments arise from being overweight or obese. He believed that an overweight person is actually carrying extra weight with him all the time, which is a burden on the person's heart as it has to pump that additional amount of blood.

He believed in a healthy life style. In his view, the most neglected asset of a human being was his body. A person buys and sells various assets during his lifetime like cars, houses, household appliances etc. He cares for them very much. Even if there is a slight scratch on his new car, he gets disturbed and wants to get it repaired immediately. He constructs a new house with all the luxury that he can afford, however, when it comes to the upkeeping of his body, he does precious little. According to him, one of the biggest wonders in this world was that everyone knows very well the importance of a regular physical exercise, yet very few actually practice it. People don't really care for their bodies unless they get some shocks from the doctor. And ironically, while all other material assets are acquired and sold, their body is the only asset they carry with them till their last breath.

Then he used to have nutritious breakfast and go to the school. He was very satisfied to see the eagerness of the students to learn new things. And the expressions when they understood that concept made him extremely happy.

He used to come home in the afternoon and have lunch comprising of fresh vegetable salad, Dal and roti. He had made it a rule in his house to use less oil for cooking and use as many green leafy vegetables as possible. According to him, food should be used as a means of survival and not as material indulgence. He loved to have a nap for just an hour which kept him active for rest of the day. In the evening, he used to go for a 4 km walk. On the way, he used to meet people in groups and he joined them occasionally if there was any interesting news to share.

Evenings were very special for Pankaj and his family. They used to sit in the pooja room and recite some bhajans based on which day of the week it was. Some neighbors also joined them in this ritual every day. The lamps in the pooja room and the divine fragrance of the incense sticks used to make the atmosphere very pure and sacrosanct. Then Pankaj used to read a text of about 8-10 pages from ancient scriptures like Ramayana, Mahabharata, Bhagwad Gita or the Upanishads. His belief was that these scriptures were not meant to be read after retirement but to be read, understood and followed on a daily basis for a balanced life style. The preaching in these books is very relevant today also and can be applied to every situation we face in our daily life.

He had a light dinner at 8 pm and used to watch the news on television for some time. He retired for the day at around 9.30 pm. Every night he slept, he thanked God that he had passed another day of his life in a peaceful and happy manner. He had no worldly desire left in him. He just had one aspiration . . . to educate as many children as possible and to be as much useful to those around him.

Once, Pankaj was sitting with the sarpanch of the village to discuss the expansion of his school. He had by now educated several hundred students making them eligible to pursue higher education in nearby towns and cities.

His syllabus of primary education was not just scholastic learning required to pass the exam and obtain eligibility for higher studies. It was also to make them a good human being. He regretted the fact that today's education system was limited only to manufacturing literate people year after year, who could read and write but could not think in a manner beneficial to the society or mankind. They were becoming literate but not educated in the true sense.

The sarpanch, Vasudev Rao appreciated Pankaj's ideology very much. He also envied the cult status earned by Pankaj in Shantinagar. Even though Vasudev Rao was the sarpanch, somehow, Pankaj was given more respect by the villagers. Pankaj's views were very much sought before taking any major decision concerning the village matters. There was an implicit faith in every villager's mind that Pankaj could never think in the lesser interests of the villagers.

Vasudev Rao asked Pankaj, 'Pankaj bhai, one question has been cropping up in my mind again and again . . . and that is, why are you doing all this?'

Pankaj was surprised at this sudden unclear question. 'Doing what?' He asked.

Vasudev Rao realized that Pankaj was not a mind reader to know what was going on in his mind before he blurted out a question related to his thoughts.

Vasudev Rao smiled and said, 'Sorry that was an incomplete question. What I meant was, why are you spending your life in this small village when you could have easily settled in Mumbai earning lots of money and enjoying life with that money . . .'

Pankaj looked at him meaningfully and said, 'Vasudev Rao, I am very much enjoying my life here. Why do you get a feeling that I am not? And with regards to the city life, what is left in the city life these days? There are only concrete jungles with high levels of pollution. You cannot even breathe fresh air there. The life is controlled by mechanical clocks with limited space for emotions or feelings. People are in a race to achieve nothing. They are just running day after day. They do not know where they are heading, but they cannot afford to wait and analyze the route, whether it is taking them to their desired destination at all.'

Vasudev Rao was intently listening.

Pankaj continued, 'Talking about enjoyment, how do you define enjoyment? Is it only in earning more money and living a life of luxuries? If that was the case, the richest people in this world would be the happiest people as well. But we all know very well that, that is not the case. This is because happiness and enjoyment are not linked to the material possessions and wealth. It is purely a state of mind. It is a person's choice whether he wants to feel happy or not. People wrongly interpret that circumstances make people happy or unhappy.'

Pankaj took a long pause. As if continuing a thought from his mind said, 'The world needs to change Vasudev Rao, the way it is going, it will not lead anywhere.'

Vasudev Rao was surprised to see a sudden change in the topic.

Pankaj continued as if speaking to himself, 'People these days are valuing the wrong things. They seem to have lost the ability to judge good and bad things in life. Rather, they are slowly changing the definition of good and bad in the society. What was bad yesterday and was frowned upon is being considered good and done with pride in public today.'

Vasudev Rao thought something and as if bringing Pankaj back to the original point of discussion said, 'But how can you contribute in changing the world by sitting in this small village?'

Pankaj deeply thought for a while and said, 'Yes, Vasudev Rao, the change can happen from a small village. All it takes is faith, passion and patience. I have faith in what I am doing. I am very passionate about doing it and I am fully aware that the results of my efforts would require a few years or even decades to reflect in the society.'

'You see the big mango tree over there'? Pankaj said, pointing to a huge tree near them. 'The seed of this tree was sown by someone over a hundred years ago. When he planted this tree, he was not sure whether it would really sprout or not. He was also not expecting to eat mangoes from this tree very soon, as it would take years for the tree to grow and bear fruits. He also probably was aware that he may or may not eat the fruits from this tree. Yet he planted it and today we see a fully grown fruit bearing tree serving the people with delicious fruits year after year.'

Vasudev Rao appreciated the thought process about the mango tree yet was a little confused about how it related to Pankaj and the subject of discussion. But he did not ask him, as it would have broken Pankaj's thought process and also exposed his ignorance in understanding the link between the two subjects.

Pankaj said, 'Similarly, my actions are helping transform the lives of hundreds of students of Shantinagar year after year. These students grow and go to nearby towns and cities for higher studies. In the process, they are spreading the good moral and ethical values taught to them. They are actually 'living' the good values inculcated in them and in a way propagating them in the society. Some of them may turn teachers and spread these righteous values in a much faster manner by giving it to hundreds of students year after year. And this way, over few years, say two generations, there would be many people around the world who value right things in life. These people would choose the right priorities and shall only adopt fair means in all their dealing in personal and professional lives. The world would turn a bit better definitely with these people around.'

Vasudev Rao was overwhelmed at the ideas of Pankaj and also wondered if ever the world may really become a utopian place to live in.

CHAPTER 7

One day, while Vikram was giving a lecture on motivation to the senior management team of a software company, he realized that there was a young guy sitting in the room restlessly. He was constantly moving in his seat, looking at his watch as if he was worried about something.

Vikram noticed his behavior for some time and then asked him, 'Yes, Mr. Young blood, any problem? You seem to be thinking of something . . .'

Mr. Young blood felt apologetic for being caught for not paying attention in the class and said, 'Sir, I was advised to leave my mobile and blackberry outside for attending this training. And I am worried how many mails and calls I would miss during this period . . . !'

Vikram smiled and said, 'Ok, assume that there would be 20 mails and 4 calls missed by you in these 2 hours. What is going to happen? Hell is not going to fall, right?'

Mr. Young blood said, 'True, but they could be important. Some of them might need my urgent attention; you know . . . I handle a very large portfolio in my company.'

Vikram looked at him with pity and said, 'Look, I agree with you that you hold a very responsible position in your company. But how much of those responsibilities have you delegated? The fact that you look worried without your mobile and blackberry suggest that you are suffering from the 'connectivity syndrome'. You feel very insecure without your gadgets connecting you with the world.'

Mr. Young blood was listening, yet not fully comfortable.

Vikram continued, 'What is the maximum that can happen outside? There would be a fire? An earthquake? A Tsunami? There are people there who can take care of the emergencies. It is wrong on your part to imagine that without you the rescue operations would be less effective. The world survives very well without individuals.'

Now Mr. Young blood was realizing the seriousness of Vikram's words.

Vikram said, 'For something which has not happened outside, you spent your time worrying. The same time you could have spent listening to me in the class and you would have been more knowledgeable.'

Now Mr. Young blood was attentive to every word spoken by Vikram.

Vikram now looked at the whole class and said, 'How many of you carry your mobiles and blackberry when you go to attend a marriage ceremony? Or a musical concert?'

Almost everyone raised their hands.

Vikram said, 'Many times, we miss to enjoy simple moments of life because we are busy working. The life passes by us every second. How many times you have taken your spouse outside for a dinner and attended official lengthy phone calls while having the dinner? How many times did you dampen the enthusiasm of your child when he is narrating some interesting incident happened in his school that day, and you interrupt him saying that you are busy in office work and that you will listen to him later . . . ?'

'Guys, please do not mix work with your family. Your family needs a space in your life which is not substitutable by any other sphere. They deserve that space from you. You may give your life for the company, but what will the company give you in your times of need? Just imagine, you are paralyzed and bed ridden. Will the company continue to pay you month after month? No. But your family will continue to be concerned about you; they will take care of you and be with you till you recover.'

The class was listening silently and imagining the scene within them.

Vikram took a long pause and said, 'God has given all of us exactly 24 hours in a day. Not a second less and not a second more. It is up to us, how we are going to utilize it. The people who utilize it efficiently become successful in their life, while others are termed as losers.'

At this point of time, Vikram looked at the faces of each of the attentively listening participants and said, 'Ok, let me ask you a simple question. Who is a 'successful person' according to you? Please write it on a piece of paper and hand it over to me. Don't write your names, so that your identity is not disclosed. That will also remove your inhibitions about revealing your true feelings to others.'

Everyone went into deep thoughts as they were struggling to write who they considered as a 'successful person'. After about twenty minutes, all the chits were with Vikram. He collected them and started writing on the board from each paper.

There were many interesting points written like:

> A businessman with increasing profits year after year,
> A family man who spends quality time with his wife and children,
> A stock market investor who consistently makes profits,
> A person who has enough money and time to travel around the world,
> A person who is healthy and exercises regularly
> Etc.

By now, all the participants were wondering about all points except the one written by them. They were realizing that the definition of a 'successful person' could vary so much among the people in a classroom.

Vikram said, 'Dear friends, these points reflect your attitude. These points reflect your ideology. These points reflect your ambitions in life. In short, these points say about who you are.'

Then he took one effective pause and said, 'But do you know what is the actual meaning of successful person? A successful person is one who can adapt to changing circumstances. Darwin's theory of ecology also suggests 'survival of the fittest'. And the fittest according to Darwin is one who is flexible and can adjust with the changing environment. However, according to Bhagwad Gita, a successful person is one who remains balanced in different situations in his life. He does not get flattered by praise and does not get demoralized by the criticism. He appears same in happiness and sadness. He behaves similarly in victory and defeat. His feelings are same in all the varying conditions in life. Bhagwad Gita refers to such a man as 'Sthita Pradnya . . . !

Therefore, a successful person is one who can become a Sthita Pradnya.'

*   *   *

Amit was very much surprised to hear the name of Srikant as the minister who is demanding more money for approvals. He had mixed feelings. He wondered how his childhood friend had become corrupt with the system. He also wondered how powerful Srikant had become, that without his approval, Amit could not start his factory even though he had all the money in the world.

Amit wondered whether Srikant would give him a discount once he came to know that it was his factory. Amit also wondered whether Srikant would be embarrassed to ask him money. He was thinking about how to approach the discussion on this sensitive subject.

Amit and Sundara Rajan went to the office of Srikant Joglekar. Sundara Rajan filled up the visitor's log. They were asked to sit on the plush sofa while the secretary went inside to inform Srikant about their arrival. After about half an hour of waiting, the secretary signaled them to go inside the office of Minister Srikant Joglekar.

Amit and Sundara Rajan entered the big office of Srikant. It was easily a 600 sq.ft office studded with various pieces of artifacts at corners and walls adorned with modern art paintings. Srikant sat in the executive chair talking to someone on phone. He had become fat now and his face looked plump. He wore the traditional white khadi dress with grey half sleeve jacket over it.

He ended the conversation by saying a few words like 'Ok . . . right' and then 'bye . . .'

He looked at the two visitors. His expressions revealed that he seemed to recognize Amit, but was not sure.

Amit removed his confusion at once and said, 'Hi Srikant, how are you?'

Sundara Rajan was shocked to see his boss talking to the minister by addressing him with his first name.

Srikant now recognized Amit after Amit spoke to him, and replied pointing a finger at him, 'Amit Saxena? What a surprise . . . ! How are you? It has been a long time man . . .'

Amit felt happy that Srikant had not only recognized him but also showed no signs of power going to his head. He signaled Sundara Rajan to leave them alone so that they could talk freely like friends who met after so many years.

Srikant asked his secretary to bring two cups of coffee and asked, 'Amit how is life? Where are you now?'

Amit said, 'Well Srikant, as you are aware, I had this idea of business from our childhood. I initially took up a marketing job and grew in that. However, after a few years, I thought of working for myself and I started my own company. With the knowledge I had gained over the years, with the support of the company I worked for, the wishes of good friends and God's blessings I have come to a stage where I feel happy to have travelled all the distance. It has been a worthwhile journey thus far.'

Srikant was looking at him with admiration in his eyes clearly visible.

Amit said, 'Leave that . . . but what is this? You have become a big leader . . . how did you do this?'

Srikant looked at his office from wall to wall, as if to feel his position before he spoke and said, 'Amit, it has been a long journey for me too. As you are aware, I was jobless for a few months after our graduation. We moved to Delhi and I was looking for a job. It was then that I came in contact with my mentor, my Guru . . . Sukhram ji. I grew up under his blessing and support. Today I am recognized as one of the future leaders of our party. And I am happy about it.'

Both of them looked impressed with each other's achievements in life so far.

After some more of the gratifying conversation, Srikant asked, 'Well, Amit, now tell me what brings you to my office?'

Amit hesitated to state the things bluntly and said, 'Srikant, I am starting a new plant in Gurgaon, for which I need approval from the environmental ministry. And the approvals are stuck up . . . as the drawings and plans are not very clear to the ministry . . .'

Amit had tried to be modest and told the official version before broaching the uncomfortable question. He also felt that Srikant was aware of the 'approval process' and was only feigning ignorance to avoid the blunt truth.

Srikant reacted, 'Are the applications with us? Surely there would be reasons for holding up then. You know, these environmental issues are keeping the world on a boil these days. Every day a new 'fact' is discovered and it alters the entire perspective of the earth's longevity. Some time they say that global warming is melting the ice blocks in Antarctica and simultaneously there are unexplainable cold winters in Europe . . .'

Amit thought for a while and said, 'Srikant, let us get to the facts. I was told that you guys have doubled your demands for this approval. And that is the reason why you have withheld the approval. Is that so?'

Srikant was slightly embarrassed at this exposure of facts. He had known about this, but by saying a sentence or two on general topics earlier during the conversation, he was actually trying to figure out how to say the truth. But now, faced with the truth, he had no option but to confirm the same.

Srikant looked at the writing pad on his table for a moment, then glanced out of the window through the semi transparent curtains and then spoke to Amit.

Srikant said, 'Yes Amit! We need more money for this approval.'

Amit was shocked at this candid confession. He did not know what to say.

Srikant continued, 'You know Amit, politics is a dirty business. On the face of it you see all the power, and hype. But behind it is actually a very dark and relatively unknown world.'

Amit was further shocked at this continued expression of truth. He did not expect that Srikant would blatantly unravel the truth like this.

Amit did not know how to react. Could he ask the reasons why? Could he bargain? Could he object paying this amount?

After some pause Amit asked, 'But Srikant, you know very well that our plans are correct. Our systems are perfect. Still you ask for more money. Is that correct?'

Srikant appeared as though he hesitated to say something.

Finally he said, 'Amit, in politics, there are no relations and friends. There is just money and power. Power brings money and money brings more power.'

Amit was listening.

Srikant continued, 'Today every politician in this country is out to make as much money as possible during his term. Every day counts. Every deal that is approved counts. No one is sure about their future. Today we are in power . . . Tomorrow we may not be.'

Srikant was in an unusual mood of revealing the dark secrets of his political life to Amit. He walked across and took a few paces as if to compose himself before continuing with his talk.

Srikant's tone also was changed now. It was more of a confession than words spoken with authority by a minister. He said, 'Do you know how much price I had to pay for this? I paid almost Rs. 100 Crores to get this portfolio. What is wrong if I want to get my money back . . . .'

Amit was surprised. He said, 'Do you mean that this is a business?'

Srikant replied without hesitation, 'Yes, of course. Today, politics is the biggest business industry in India. It is the richest industry with thousands of Crores of transactions happening during one term of five years. It is the most powerful sector where you can directly control and influence the lives of millions of people across India. It is the only field where you will be in the media day in and day out for anything you do right or wrong.'

Amit was too surprised to hear these honest words from a politician. He said, 'Srikant, What about your moral values? They have no place in front of money?'

Srikant smiled and said, 'Amit, I had a lot of moral values and still continue to hold them. But when a system gets corrupt, you cannot do anything. One person is too helpless to effect a change in a massive system.'

Amit interrupted, 'But that does not mean that you too join them, right?'

Srikant looked meaningfully at Amit and said, 'How do you think I can survive without joining them? They will not allow me to be in power even for a single day. Actually I was not like this before. You know me very well from our childhood days. But over the years, they have moulded me into their system.'

Amit said, 'Do you think that blaming the system will absolve you of your sins? Did you also not show your consent at every step till you reached this stage?'

Srikant said, 'Amit, you are right. This path has been chosen by me so I am responsible for my actions. However, there were certain factors which led me to this stage. Firstly, I was lured by the power before I got it. I used to get thrilled to see the ministers with red flashing lights go past on the roads. Luckily I got an opportunity to be a part of this. There are thousands of party workers aspiring to make it big in politics. Only a few can come up. So, that was an achievement in itself.'

'As regards the morality is concerned, I had to compromise, since it is an occupational hazard. You cannot live in water without making friendship with fish. I convinced my mind that this was the requirement of the job. And why not? Who does not want to make more money in this world? What is wrong if I chose to earn more money?'

Amit interrupted, 'But the money earned through illegal means will not stay long. That will go away in unexpected manner through some means or other. At least it will not bring you happiness, for sure.'

Srikant laughed now and said, 'Amit, these are all the talks of wisdom they used to tell in olden days. Do you find any honest person rich today? Has any person who has earned all his wealth only through legal means ever lived in a posh bunglow? Do you mean all these rich people are suffering? These are all the talks intended to dissuade the people from doing anything illegal.'

Amit had begun to slightly hate Srikant now. Apparently Srikant was noticing the change in the expressions on Amit's face. He said, 'Amit, let me ask you one thing. You are also earning money in hordes. What is difference between you and me? You are in your business and I am in my business . . .'

Amit said, 'There is a big difference, Srikant. Agreed, that I work hard day and night to grow my empire. I toil every day to increase my bottom line. But remember, all the money earned by me is through legal means. I do not earn a single paisa through illegal means.'

Srikant said, 'And what difference it makes? Money is money, right?'

Amit said, 'No Srikant, you are mistaken. The money earned through illegal means may give you luxuries, but it cannot guarantee you happiness. It may enable you to buy the best bed in the world, but it cannot guarantee you sleep.'

'It will keep pricking your conscience every single minute you are awake. It will lower your self esteem. It will keep nagging at the back of your mind that this is not rightfully earned money.'

There was a long pause in the room. They both realized that they had already stated whatever they had to say. There was nothing more to add. And they were sticking to their own viewpoint even after this long argument.

The mutual admiration these two friends had just a while ago was transformed into some kind of a friction. They were not angry at each other. They just realized that their ideologies differed on certain prime issues.

After a few moments of pause, Amit asked Srikant, 'Ok Srikant, any discount for my project?' There was a touch of sarcasm in his tone.

Srikant said, 'Amit do you think I have fallen so much that I want to make money from my friends also? Well, I might have fallen in your eyes a bit today, but I am not such a rogue as to willfully charge you as well. However I still need to collect some money from you.'

Amit was puzzled. This was a contradictory statement.

Srikant said, 'Well Amit, do you know that the money that I collect from you and others is shared among many people in the system? A large portion of it goes to the high command. They know the rapid industrialization taking place in Gurgaon. That is why they have fixed a monthly sum as target to be sent to them irrespective of the proposals sanctioned by me. If I do not take any money from you, I have to pay from my pocket to fill up the gap. And I am sure you would not want me to pay on your behalf, right?'

Amit was stunned. This was an organized mafia where there were only sharks. No one was spared. He started feeling pity for Srikant now that he was working in an environment which not only corrupted him but also ensured that he stayed that way. It was more like the famous dialogue of the Bollywood villains who say that there are many ways of entering but no route of exit.

For some reason, these two grown up men became emotional and hugged each other. It was as though they were silently accepting the unpleasant circumstances with a helpless feeling that they could not do anything to change it.

CHAPTER 8

Vikram had a hectic schedule since last few weeks. He had travelled to Far East, then Europe and lastly US. He had been giving corporate training now and his popularity had extended worldwide. He had set up a small office as well, with a staff of 16 members. They were the ones who scheduled his appointments, managed his accounts, publicity, marketing and publications.

He often wondered how he had changed his line from a factory engineer to a high flying motivational speaker. His knowledge of mythology made him a unique speaker who blended the modern management theories with the mythological concepts seamlessly. His outlook changed drastically after he started meeting people and addressed their issues.

He realized that many people in this world have good potential but do not have the courage to take bold decisions in life. If these people take even some calculated risks they could become more successful than what they were, but they do not have the courage to do so. Financial stability was the biggest factor which adversely affected many people's careers.

He observed that the Indian education system created lakhs of graduates every year without teaching them how to be successful in their lives. These graduates became part of the crowd on the streets searching for jobs. Be it marketing; call centre, advertising, insurance sales etc. Because of the social pressures, these young souls took up whichever job came their way first and they continued in the same profession irrespective of whether they enjoyed it or not. And soon they reach a stage in which their CV is dominated by their current field which forces them to continue in it. The wise among them grow in that field only. But the majority languishes in the listless jobs without any growth, as their performance is mediocre.

There are very few examples, where people have shown courage to change their profession or career mid way. It requires lot of guts, financial support, self-motivation and passion to change careers after spending few years in it. And those who did, generally succeeded. After all, an old saying 'fortune favors the brave' confirms this fact.

By looking at the audience Vikram could now identify and separate the really interested candidates from the ones who attended his programmes by force. He had seen many varieties of candidates in his classes. There were the genuinely interested ones, who wanted to take as much positive values from the class and implement it for their benefit. Then there were those who attended the training because their company nominated them. Vikram also knew that among the nominees, there were some candidates who were useless for their organization and were sent because the company had paid the fees for specific number of seats and the executive originally intended to be trained could not be spared because of exigencies.

Vikram was disappointed to note that many companies still did not give enough importance to the concept of training. Many Corporates considered training as a wasteful expenditure, while the candidates behaved as though the training programs are a break from their stressed up routine jobs.

The frequent travelling had taken its toll on Vikram's personal life. Initially, he used to absolutely enjoy the air travels, accommodation in good hotels or guest houses, meeting different people every time, giving motivational lectures on various subjects etc however, after his marriage, he started feeling the pinch of it. He could not curtail his commitments, as it was his source of income and he knew that it was not a regular source guaranteed for several years. Tomorrow if another high profile management guru arrives on the scene, the world would run behind him. So, Vikram generally did not refuse any requests unless the dates clashed with an existing program.

Vineetha initially adjusted with his schedules. She would take his absence in her stride. She learnt the various traditional forms of art like embroidery, painting etc. But after few months, she was bored of this life. She was married, but living without her husband for almost 2-3 weeks in a month.

Once she asked Vikram whether he could do anything to stop his travels. He just laughed and said, 'What is the problem? We are earning money. I enjoy giving motivational lectures. You have your freedom. Live as you like. There are no constraints for you. Learn the art that you always wanted to. Indulge in the activities that interest you and you will enjoy life.' She realized that he was giving a lecture as if it was a motivational class.

Probably that was where Vikram was mistaken. He never really bothered to explore the true feelings of his wife. He always thought that it was a common thing for wives to complain about their husband's extended travel itinerary which was slowly drifting them apart.

That is why, when Vikram came back from US after spending well over a month and a half outside, there was a storm brewing in his home. Vineetha was in a state of semi depression. She was unhappy about his long absence and more so about the fact that he never tried to understand her feelings about his absence.

Vikram reached home and as usual hugged Vineetha. He was tired but happy to be home. She was looking forward to his arrival and had prepared the food of his liking. He got freshened up and they had a good dinner. They went for a long drive after dinner.

Vineetha said, 'Vikram, how many more years we will spend like this? I mean you're travelling and we staying apart . . .'

Vikram said,' Oh darling, this is my life now. I can't be away from all this. You know I have gained such fame and popularity only because I am able to motivate people and their performance improves after they attend my lectures/seminars.'

Vineetha was not impressed. She said, 'That is true, Vikram, but you do have a personal life of your own, right?'

Vikram acted confused. He said, 'Yes, so what about it? It is a wonderful life.'

Vineetha said, now more directly, 'Sometimes I feel that you are improving the lives of other people, but not caring enough about your own life. Don't you feel that you also should enjoy life?'

Vikram was slowly getting the gist of it. He said, 'who said I am not enjoying my life? I very much enjoy every moment of it . . .'

Vineetha said, 'And what about so many moments you spend regularly away from me? Do you enjoy those moments too?'

Vikram was in a fix. He could neither say yes nor say no.

He said, 'Dear Vineetha, life is like that. You do not get everything you want in life. Imagine if I spend 24 hours a day and 365 days in a year with you and earn nothing. Will that bring happiness to us?'

Vineetha said, 'Agreed Vikram, but there has to be an end to this somewhere. With each day, we are getting older and older. The day we can spend today together cannot be equated with a day we can spend together at the age of 60. Today we have some thoughts, some ambitions, some capabilities, some aspirations, some dreams and some hopes. At the age of 60, they will be very different from what they are now. There will be several limitations and restrictions. We may not be able to do many things which we can do today. Our priorities then will be to maintain good health above everything else. In those days, a day spent without any illness is going to be the happiest day for us.'

Vikram thought about it. For a moment he felt that she was giving him a motivational lecture.

Vikram said, 'I agree with you Vineetha. Let me see, how we can manage this change of reducing my travel commitments . . .'

Vineetha was happy that she could drive the point home today. Yet she was not confidant that Vikram would do something about it soon. She was only hopeful that he would seriously consider her statements and do something about it.

*   *   *

Amit was expanding his business in different domains and also in geographical zones. He was now touching the lives of a common man in some way or other every day. His business was robust, with increasing profit margins year after year. His bankers were happy as they were getting good business from him. His shareholders were also happy as they were getting good returns on their investments on sustained basis.

Amit was very happy today as his son, Aniket was returning from US after doing his post graduation in business management. He was eagerly waiting for this moment, as he wanted to see his son taking some load off his shoulders. And it is always a pleasure for any person to start delegating the powers to his son.

Amit had himself gone to the airport to receive Aniket, the future successor of his business empire. Aniket arrived amidst much fanfare. Amit had organized a royal welcome for his son, with garlands and flowers showered on him as he came out of the arrivals.

Amit wanted his son to learn all the features of his company. Therefore, he inducted Aniket into his company as a Management Trainee. The HR director was surprised at this move from Amit. If Amit wanted, he could have made Aniket the Managing Director straightaway, but he did not do so.

The staff felt very awkward when Aniket was around. They were uncomfortable in discussing employee welfare issues in the presence of Aniket, yet they were very helpful to him and clarified whatever doubts he had. Aniket was a keen observer and did not leave any opportunity to learn the job requirements which he was assigned to.

Amit planned to give exposure to Aniket in each level in the organization, so that he learns the duties, roles and challenges of every position in the company. Thereafter, he would be given a promotion every 6 months. So, he would climb the ladder in the company through each grade viz. officer, senior officer, Assistant Manager, Deputy Manager, Manager, Senior Manager, Assistant General Manager, Deputy General Manager, General Manager, Vice President, President in around 5-7 years . . .

One day Amit called Aniket to his cabin and asked him how he felt about working in the plant. Actually he wanted to talk about his expansion plans and see if Aniket could add any value in it. But Aniket's body language rather surprised him. He seemed to have come for the discussion more by force than by choice. He wondered whether he was imposing himself too much on him. But however hard he tried to remember, he was never too strict on him.

Amit said, finally, 'What happened Aniket? You are not feeling well?'

Aniket replied in an unexcited fashion, 'Nothing dad. It is just the work pressure.'

Amit was surprised to note that Aniket was getting tired out of work pressure.

He said, 'Good my son. This is the age for you to work hard. Learn the business well so that you can manage it in future.'

Aniket hesitated to say something and then said, 'Dad, it is not the pressure that is tiring me. It is the lack of interest in this work that is putting me off.'

Amit was shocked to hear this from his son.

He said, 'What happened? You find it boring? This is actually so exciting . . . you have an opportunity to learn the business plans . . . you meet new customers . . . you enter new territories . . . you compete with new players in the marketplace . . . you devise new strategies to overcome the challenges . . . does this not excite you?'

Aniket looked calmly sideways and said, 'No.' Apparently, he could not see in Amit's eyes.

Amit was deeply disappointed. He had built this empire from scratch and was proud of it. He was now looking forward to take a backseat and enjoy overseeing the strategic affairs of the company leaving the day to day operations to his son. And here his son was plainly informing him that he was not interested in his business.

Amit said, 'But Aniket, I have built this business brick by brick with my sweat. Lot of effort has gone in making this business what it is today. And you say you are not interested in it?'

Aniket was not moved by this passionate speech of his father. He said in a reconciliatory note, 'It is not that dad. Please do not misunderstand me. I fully appreciate your efforts in making this business successful. I also deeply respect you and your values. But at the same time, I have to be honest in letting you know that this business does not interest me. I may continue working here, and get promotions as you have planned for me, but finally I may not be able to perform as per your expectations, as I am not passionate about this business . . .'

Amit was still reeling under shock. He said, 'Then what is your passion, Aniket?' There was a touch of sarcasm in his tone when he uttered the word, passion.

Aniket again hesitated to say something and then finally said, 'Dad, I would like to work in films. I want to be an actor.'

This was a much bigger shock for Amit. He had not expected that his son would keep such hopeless ambitions. Agreed that he was a handsome looking young man, but so are thousands of people landing in Mumbai every day in search for a niche in Bollywood. And he knew very well that Bollywood was a highly deceptive arena where merit alone did not count in becoming a successful person.

Amit said, 'Do you know Aniket that behind every successful star there are lakhs and lakhs of unsuccessful people who are almost equal in all respect to the stars but do not have the luck on their side? Do you know that many of these unsuccessful people go into cycles of depression once their dreams are shattered? Are you aware that this industry is not very high on moral values?' Amit spelled out whatever negative he could think of about Bollywood at that moment.

Aniket said, 'But dad, why should we look at the negative side only? You yourself have taken big risks in business to come to this position. I am also doing the same. So what's wrong with it?'

Amit was at a loss of words at this irrational logic of his son. He said, 'Yes beta, but take risks where there are at least some chances of success and the outcome is largely based on your efforts. The risks pay off in such cases, not in all.'

Aniket again said like a child, 'But dad, I am confident that I can make it big in Bollywood. I am sure that I will be a star one day. You will be a proud father . . .'

Amit was not listening to him anymore. His mind was going numb. His aspirations were shattered in front of his eyes. His dream of seeing his son make dynamic business moves was going to remain a dream . . . !

*   *   *

After meeting Amit there was some change in Srikant's attitude. He wondered how he had changed over the years. He was now fully embroiled in a system where accepting bribes was a routine thing. A place where people were measured by power and money they had, more than the values they possessed. He went into soul searching as to what changed him. He distinctly remembered the first time he accepted a bribe. That was when as a municipal counselor he had to give an approval for the construction of a theatre in his area of jurisdiction. He felt very guilty of accepting the money then. But his secretary had advised him that it was a very normal thing and it would have been very unusual if he did not accept the money.

Thereafter, he started accepting the money for every approval given by him. He had started focusing on the potential money he would get by approving a particular file, rather than what the proposal was for. Of course, his power grew with the positions held by him in the party and the governments. And with that the money he earned also increased manifold.

Sometimes he felt that the society was responsible for all the corruption. If the people do not give money and stand united, what could the corrupt officers do? They cannot do anything. It is when some rich people who have enough money start offering bribes for getting the works done in a quicker way the officers get used to it and demand money when not offered. And the cycle continues.

He was also aware of the risks involved in taking bribes. If anytime one gets caught accepting money, then his future gets affected badly. He may have to resign from his current position as a first measure to pacify the public. Then comes the enquiry. If the enquiry results prove the person guilty, then there could be a jail term. He had known many of his friend politicians from all the parties, who had bribed the enquiry commissions, and reduced the severity of the findings. They spent few months in the jail and came out to live another day. People also had a short lived memory, with so many events happening daily to provide the much needed distraction. People forgot the past quickly.

The media was getting hungry for sensational news. There were some power houses controlling the media but as the media industry was growing fast, the competition was high and the stakes were also getting higher.

Srikant's personal life was not a very satisfied one. As he was required to spend a lot of time for his party affairs and official tours, he could neither spend qualitative nor quantitative time with his family. As a result, his children had grown in an atmosphere of richness and power. The essential values of kindness, humility, respect etc were grossly missing in them.

His son could barely finish his graduation as he was too weak in studies. He was regularly in news for all the wrong reasons. Once he was caught drunk in a marriage party when he picked up a fight with a person who accidentally stamped on his foot. On another occasion, the police were called by his college principal when he openly defied the lecturers and abused them for not helping him in copying during the exams. The local newspapers had all carried these news reports forcing him to give some explanations to the media later on.

His daughter was also not interested in studies and was only focusing on fashion and beauty. The amount spent by her on the accessories was too high. It was not that he could not afford it, but inside his mind, he was not sure whether she was on the right track.

For the first time after meeting Amit, he was introspecting whether he himself was on the right track. He had earned a lot of money and experienced power as well. But was that the aim of his life? Where was this road leading him to? As far as he imagined, he was in a race where he had to keep running or else he would be overtaken by his competitors within the party.

There seemed to be no exit from this 'chakravyuha'.

CHAPTER 9

Once while Vikram was in Delhi, he received a call from his neighbor that his wife had been hospitalized as she was not well. He was shocked and wanted to know more details but the neighbors did not reveal much. They just said that she was stable now and that he could complete his assignment and return as early as possible.

However, he was too disturbed at this news and caught the next flight to Mumbai. He suddenly started remembering her intensely like never before. He remembered her innocent smile, her caring attitude, her gracious presence and ever happy mood. He also remembered her request to him recently to cut down on his tours and spend more time with her. Was she aware that something was going to happen to her, when she spoke about that to him? He had no idea. Only thing he thought now was to meet her and look into her deep eyes and get lost in them. He wondered whether he was a good husband at all.

He suddenly thought that he was going too adrift in thoughts and that it could be a simple illness. Why should he worry so much? When emotions take over a person, logic usually takes a back seat. Rarely a person can think logic when high on emotions.

He reached Mumbai and went straight to the hospital. He went to her room and saw her. Her face was looking pale and she was asleep. The doctor was standing beside her and explaining something to the neighbors who were still there. Tears started rolling down Vikram's eyes for no reason. Probably it was because he had never seen his wife in this condition before. He had always seen her smiling and lightening the mood. Her smile would make him forget any worry in the world. And there she lay on the bed not smiling.

The neighbors rushed to support and console him. They said that she was fine now and there was no reason to worry. But he was still not clear as to what had happened to her all of a sudden. When he had left 4 days back, she was fine, in her usual spirits. He wanted to enquire more details about her illness from the doctor but first he wanted to be with her, near her. He went near the bed and sat on the edge. He took her hand in his and looked at her face. She seemed to recognize the touch and opened her eyes slowly. There were mixed feelings on her face. She was happy to see him, but was not very happy to present herself in this condition to him. As if he understood her feelings, he patted her hand with his other hand and conveyed through his eyes that he was there now and that there was no reason to worry anymore.

She smiled faintly and closed her eyes again. Vikram sat with her hand in his hands for some more time and when he felt that she had fallen asleep, he went to the doctor's cabin. The Doctor was looking at some reports.

Vikram asked the doctor, 'Doctor, what is the problem with Vineetha?'

The doctor looked somewhat worried behind his stoic face. Doctors have an unenviable job of answering this question of anxious relatives of the patients. And they have no choice but to say the truth, however bitter it might be. God has made doctors to heal the patients but they have also been entrusted with the responsibility of giving bad news.

The doctor cleared his throat as if gaining time to decide what to say. He said, 'Mr. Vikram, Vineetha is suffering from Liver Cancer. We have detected a stage three cancer in her liver.'

Vikram felt as though the world around him had suddenly darkened. He felt extreme weakness in his body and struggled to remain seated in the chair. His throat had gone dry and his mind was going numb. He was in a state of high shock.

The doctor continued, 'Mr. Vikram, I can understand your feelings. We shall try our best to recover her from this illness, but it is going to take time.'

Vikram barely said, 'Doctor, what are the chances of her survival . . . ?'

Doctor looked at the reports once again, as if negotiating with the nature in his mind and said, 'Fifty fifty.'

Vikram did not know whether he should feel happy or sad about this. He had on numerous occasions spoke in his seminars about half glass full and half glass empty, but he was not very clear whether it was applicable here. Even if it was, he did not want to look at just the positive half side. He wanted it to be fully positive. While he professed to his students about being positive in life in any adverse conditions, he was not so sure about how he would react when it came to his personal life and his emotions. For the first time he felt that it was easier to preach than to practice the management philosophy of being motivated in difficult times.

He asked the Doctor, 'Doctor, why do people get cancer?'

The doctor now turned philosophical. He said, 'Mr. Vikram, nature has kept certain secrets and powers with her. Mankind has not been able to decipher that area as yet. One of them is cancer. The world's medicine fraternity is not yet fully clear on what causes cancer. It just happens. If we are able to detect it in early stages, we can cure it with a higher success ratio. If, however, it is detected late, then there is no cure invented as of now.'

For the first time Vikram thought that there is something called destiny. How else was he going to justify the reason why his wife got the cancer? He now also started wondering whether the 'Paap' and 'Punya' of his previous janma had anything to do with his current situation.

Vikram started missing his wife like never before. He wanted to talk to her, sit with her in their balcony and drink coffee with her. He remembered her every small gesture and suddenly started feeling a bit guilty that he was away from her for longer periods, which drove her to actually say this to him. As an ideal husband, he should have been able to understand her feeling and act on them before they were spoken with a request.

He came out of the doctor's cabin with a heavy heart almost dragging his feet. He was not sure, how he would look into Vineetha's eyes once she wakes up soon.

*   *   *

Amit had not spoken to Aniket for a week after that day, when he had declared his ambition. He was also not in his usual exuberant moods in the office these days. He was worried about his son's future. He knew that the ambition nourished by his son was not going to take him far in life. And as a loving father, this very thought made him somewhat depressed. He sometimes used to wonder, where he lacked in upbringing his son. He always provided the best of everything to Aniket. He wondered how much control a father can have over his son in his forming years when he needs to possess the quality to separate the good from the bad and have right priorities in life. However much a father can desire, ultimately, it depends on the son to take right decisions and progress in life.

But then, love is one thing the world survives on. The love for his son made him lose the animosity he had developed over the fanatic ambition nourished by Aniket. He started accepting the reality on ground instead of worrying over how it differed from his ideas and imaginations. He started talking to him again, more sympathetically, and tried to understand him better.

Amit said cheerfully, "So Aniket, since when you had this ambition of acting in films? You never spoke of it in your childhood . . . ?"

Aniket felt happy at seeing that his father was discussing about his ambition positively. He said, 'Actually I was thrilled since my childhood to see the Hindi movies. The hero in the movies is adorned by all the audience. It is actually unreal, I know. The audience is also clever to know that what is portrayed is not practical most of the time, yet they appreciate the performance. I want to act and be appreciated for my performance.'

Amit realized that the passion for acting in this boy had now reached levels beyond reversal. Either he goes ahead with his passion to act in films, or he would simply be dejected for life. Amit thought, if this is what destiny had in store for him, so be it. He slowly changed himself and started accepting the fact that his son wanted to act in films. At times, he even respected the passion displayed by Aniket for acting in films. He knew one thing . . . if one pursues his passion; he is bound to achieve success sooner or later. But how far this noble statement would apply here was a big question mark.

Amit contacted one of his friends Rohit Khanna who was a distributor of films. Being in the high society there was one advantage. He came across many high profile people in different spheres in various functions and events attended by the page 3 celebrities. He had known Rohit Khanna for some time now. They had met at an awards function last year. They had exchanged pleasantries then and also had bumped into each other on two occasions thereafter in parties.

Amit called Rohit on his mobile and asked him for his time to discuss about Aniket. Amit was feeling very awkward to state the purpose of his meeting, but as they say, you cannot hide the vessel when you go to a neighbor's house to borrow butter milk. Rohit was a bit surprised to hear this request, yet he obliged Amit's request and set a time the following week to meet and discuss the proposal.

Aniket was thrilled to hear that his dad was actually making some efforts to help him get into an acting career. He started respecting his father much more. At the same time, Amit was not sure whether he was doing the right thing by aiding his son to follow a listless pursuit, which would cost him a career and also affect his life style.

Amit and Aniket went to meet Rohit on the scheduled day in a 5 star hotel. A pool side table was booked for them by Amit. Aniket wore a dark grey suit and a matching tie. He was looking handsome after doing the extra make up for this meeting. He had an idea that Rohit was not the person who would give him a film, but it was necessary to impress Rohit if he had to recommend Aniket to someone.

After the initial greeting and some talk on weather and a brief pause, Rohit looked at Amit thoughtfully and said, 'Amit, are you sure Aniket wants to join films? I mean does he have the strength to bear a failure?'

Amit was taken aback at this blunt question from Rohit. He said, 'What do you mean Rohit? I think we can be more positive . . .'

Rohit said, 'Amit, sorry for being forthright . . . but there is very high level of competition these days in Bollywood. The star sons are occupying the major space and the veterans are still not calling it a day. There are thousands of new hopefuls landing in Mumbai every day from all over India to make it big in the film industry. 99.9% of them end up in frustration, depression and end up playing the role of a non-entity in a mob or pack their bags and go back.'

Amit and Aniket were silently listening to this highly demotivating opinion on the film industry by a person making a living out of it.

Rohit looked at Aniket and continued, 'Aniket, the stardom comes with a cost. The attempts to stardom also come with a cost. You need to be highly flexible with your attitude, when you are a newcomer. You need to be patient before someone actually signs you up for their film. You may not get a blockbuster project to start with. The role offered to you may not be worth anything. Remember, Amitabh Bachchan was one among the seven guys in his first film while in his first shot, Rajnikant opens a gate as a watchman in a movie. But then . . . everyone cannot become Amitabh or Rajnikant in life.'

The sudden reference of two superstars inspired Aniket. He said, 'Sir, I am very sure that I can make it big. I am ready to toil for that. I am ready to wait for the right opportunity to strike. I am ready to make any sacrifices for this to happen.'

Amit thought in his mind that Aniket had already made the biggest sacrifice in his life . . . that of his career. Because, this craze would go for at least few more years and by then if he is not successful, then it would be too late for him to attempt anything else in life. Again Amit squirmed in his mind about whether he was right in guiding his son in this direction. But he had no options in front of him. If he had to see his son happy, he needed to do this.

Rohit was somewhat surprised to see the spark and enthusiasm in Aniket. He continued, 'Aniket, to be successful in the film industry, you need two qualities essentially apart from, of course, the acting skills. You need to have the strength to bear the failure and you need to have the patience to wait for success. Without these two qualities, you would never be at peace with yourselves. Many of the Bollywood personalities who did not possess these qualities went into cycles of deep depressions and some of them committed suicide also.'

Aniket was intently listening to Rohit and nodding his head in affirmative at periodic intervals.

Rohit finally said that one of his friends, a film producer was launching a new film and was on the lookout for a fresh face. He took the collection of photographs brought by Aniket posing in different angles and said that he would pass it on to his friend with his recommendation.

That news came as a cool breeze in the oasis for Aniket. And for Amit, it was more of a relief that there was some headway to proceed in his son's pursuit of his passion.

At times, parents go to any extent just to satisfy the demands of their children.

*   *   *

Pankaj was enjoying his life, as he was living it exactly the way he desired to. He always wanted to be useful to the society and the community. According to him, anybody who lived for himself was not leading a proper life. The true satisfaction came when we are useful to people around us and are able to make the environment better than what it would have been without us.

Thinking about the environment reminded him about the real environment. He was hearing a lot these days about the environmental issues and the depleting natural resources. The petroleum reserves were getting exhausted and were estimated to last only for few more decades. That was the biggest challenge to the Research and Development Engineers of the entire automobile industry across the globe. They have to invent a new substitute for automobile fuel or else the industry would close down. He wondered how the world carried on itself in the first half of the last century with bicycles and bullock carts as main means of transportation. After all these years and modernization, it would be a disaster to have no Scooters, Cars and Airplanes.

Similarly, the coal mines were also facing the danger of a shut down by around 2050 as the coal stocks are estimated to be exhausted by then. He wondered how many workers would be left without jobs and what would happen to the thermal power plants around the world. How the nations would generate energy to meet the luxurious life style of their citizens? Because, currently a major portion of the power was generated through thermal power plants. He then wondered how the people in the last century lived in darkness without lights. And he suddenly realized that even today there were many villages in India where there was still no electricity.

And the most disturbing news he read was about the impending water scarcity in future. He was horrified to know that in future, the wars would be fought for water. That means, just as the gulf countries were the target of all politics revolving around the oil reserves in last two three decades, in the next few decades, the water rich countries would be vulnerable for threat of attack from others.

These thoughts woke up the 'ideal citizen' in him and he seriously started thinking about how to improve the situation. The country and the world should be saved from these dangers of not having enough fuel or natural resources.

He immediately started thinking about how to save these resources. There had to be a start somewhere. Agreed that the task was gigantic, yet a march of thousand miles began with a small step. In his next visit to Mumbai, he purchased several books on environment protection and started reading them to understand how this could be implemented.

He realized that it was no use investing in technology or buying costly equipments. What was required was a shift in the mindset of the people to conserve these natural resources. He needed to make people aware of the threat and then the impetus would come from within to save these natural resources.

So, in one of the Panchayat meetings, he narrated the entire story and asked the people what they would do to conserve energy. At first it was difficult for people to understand that the fresh water they were drinking from wells and river was going to be finished soon. It was a shock for them to know that all their tractors and motor cycles would be rendered useless in a few years to come. They were too worried that they may have to live in darkness. Well, they had experienced the power cuts from time to time, but always there was a respite when the power came back.

One by one people started proposing how they would contribute to this international cause affecting the mankind. Some said that they would economize on usage of water for washing clothes and bathing the cattle. Some proposed that they would switch off the lights and fans whenever not required. Some even suggested that they would switch off the tractor when it was idling for longer periods. They were happy that these measures also actually resulted in controlling their monthly expenditure.

Over a period of next few weeks, Pankaj taught them how to do rain water harvesting and also grow more vegetables and crops by improving the efficiency of farming, so that the logistics involved in transporting these goods from outside to Shantinagar was saved.

Slowly and steadily Shantinagar became self sufficient and the per capita income of the people also increased. The news of this town started appearing in the local newspapers and the regional TV channels.

And in every news item, Pankaj's name figured prominently as the change maker.

*   *   *

One day Srikant's secretary informed him that there was a delegation from US who wanted to meet Srikant to discuss on strengthening the ties between US and India on the environmental protection front. Such delegations visited India frequently from different countries as the governments all over the world wanted to do something for protecting the environment. Some did it out of choice and some did it by compulsion of the World Energy forum based on some statistics in their reports mentioning the carbon footprint or per capita garbage generation by that country. However, there were several countries who took initiatives only to gain positive mileage in public eye for electoral gains.

Srikant met the delegation at 11 am in his office as per the scheduled appointment. He had anticipated the visitors to be Americans, but the delegation comprised of two gentlemen and a lady, all Indians. During their introduction, he learnt that they were from the representative office in India, set up by a US authorized government agency. All three were in formal suits and carried their office bags apparently containing the reports and proposal documents.

Within five minutes of their conversation he learnt that they were keen to set up Effluent treatment plants in all major cities across India. This was a major initiative and would help in recycling the garbage and reusing wherever possible.

Mr. Khurana, the leader of this group was actively discussing on the way forward for this project. He explained the funding mechanism to Srikant. The US agency would fund 50% through the World Bank while the balance 50% needed to come from the Indian government. The total outlay for this project across 15 cities in India was estimated to be around Rs.1400 Crores. Khurana took out various drawings and plans from his bag to explain the concept to Srikant. It was important for him to convince Srikant about the concept, as based on his approval only the project could go ahead.

Srikant was thinking in his mind, this environment is a funny thing. While you save it you are doing 'Swartha' and also 'Paramartha' at the same time. There was Swartha, because you make money out of the project sanctions and

Paramartha, because you save the environment thereby helping the society.

The meeting ended after almost one and a half hours of discussion. The delegation left satisfied that they were able to explain the concept to Srikant and hopefully, in the next meeting they could sign the deal. The delegation looked very professional and they had done their home work properly. The fact that they had all the relevant statistics and details available with them showed that they were serious about this project to go through. Srikant wondered whether US was really interested in saving the environment or they just wanted a business and some role to play around the world in whichever capacity.

Srikant started thinking about his role in this project. There was big money in this. He guessed that this delegation was experienced and should have known that they need to make some payoffs to get going. He could earn easily around Rs.70 Crores, which was the 10% of the Indian government's share in the project. He had not earned so much money in a single deal so far. It was not that he had less money now, but money is like sea water. The more you drink, the thirstier you become. He could buy some property in UK and also start a 5 star hotel in Singapore, which he was thinking for some time now.

However, suddenly he remembered about his meeting with Amit. While talking to Amit, somehow he was reminded about his childhood. He thought of his middle class childhood and the good values instilled in him by his parents. His father used to say, it is better to earn 50 paise with honesty than one rupee with dishonesty. He was reminded about the simple yet happy life they lived in those days. The pleasure he had when his father took the family to local exhibitions and 'mela' was very high. They used to spend small amounts there on pop corn, Ice cream, some rides etc. The selection of right toys in the toy store was a bit tough task, as the cost and quality both had to be right. The children did not like the cheap toys and the costly toys they could not afford. Yet, after so much of discussions and haggling, they all used to return happily from these outings.

However, money had changed his life now. For the first time he realized that having too much money was also a problem. He felt that rich people often miss out on some simple pleasures of life. Like, he rarely went with his family for any exhibitions because every one of them had their own circle of friends. His wife used to spend most of her time with the high profile ladies like the wives of industrialists, businessmen, politicians etc. His son and daughter went with their respective friends. The house had more servants than masters. Many times, the communication between the family members used to be through the servants. Like keeping a message, requesting something, keeping updated about one's whereabouts etc. At least 2-3 days in a week, he used to have dinner alone, watched by the cook and the server. He used to remember then, how in his childhood his father ensured that all the family members had dinner together. They would compulsorily wait if someone was late for any reason. And his mother would particularly keep a watch on everyone's plate and ensure that everyone was eating properly.

He had only 3 pairs of good clothes till his mid twenties. And he used to wear them in different combination so as to give a feeling that he had actually more clothes. In reality, no one cared to look how many clothes he had, other than himself. And now, he had wardrobes full of clothes. His children had the best of fashion clothing available in the market. Once, his daughter had flown to Bangalore, just to buy a good dress, as she was told that good dresses were available in a particular shop on Commercial Street. He wondered whether his children had the same satisfaction he used to get when his parents stitched new clothes for him during 'Gudi Padwa' or 'Diwali'. He was not sure.

He did not know why, but there was some change in his overall attitude after meeting Amit. The good values in him were trying to come out. He had a craving for being a good person. He remembered how his father was respected as an honest man, in the society they lived in. He desired that kind of respect from people around him. But he knew what everyone thought of him currently. Rather it was anybody's guess, as to how he had earned these riches in short time. Definitely it was not his legal and righteous earning. He started reading the expressions on faces of people around him and got a feeling that they were all cursing him from within. At least they did not hold him in high esteem. He wanted to change it all.

He wondered why at this brilliant opportunity of earning big money he was getting all these divine thoughts about being righteous and virtuous. But then, mind is something which we have no control upon. A person could be in the noisiest place and still be at peace with himself and another person could be sitting on a silent beach and have a storm in his mind about some issue. If we really think, the external factors are hardly responsible for our state. It is what we make ourselves to be.

CHAPTER 10

Vineetha was discharged from the hospital after one week of tests and observation. She was prescribed a course of medication which involved several tablets and capsules throughout the day. No one really likes to take so many medicines in a day, but when time comes one has to. There are no likings involved when it comes to health issues.

Vikram cancelled all his engagements citing personal reasons and apologized to everyone personally over phone and mails. He wanted to spend as much time with Vineetha as possible to ensure that every effort is made to save her. He felt extremely apologetic that not long ago she had to literally express to him that he was not spending enough time with her and now he was doing so, but in entirely different environment and conditions. Time is a cruel thing which sometimes makes unimaginable things happen to people and they have no option but to live through those difficult moments.

Vikram wanted to make her feel comfortable and lively so that she would forget her illness. He brought home several good books, magazines, DVDs of good old classic movies which she liked and CDs of old music of her choice. He spent most of the time with her watching TV, or sitting in the balcony of their house watching the traffic below, or sitting on the terrace in the evenings sipping tea and watching the sun set in far western skies. They played Chess, Carom board, Playing cards, etc.

One day, she asked him, 'Vikram, I am really happy and thankful that you are taking so much care of me . . . !'

Vikram did not know what to say. His emotions ran high and eyes became slightly moist. He said, 'Oh my dear, I love you. I feel happy to be of help to you. I want you to be happy . . . always . . .'

Vineetha said, 'Yes Vikram, I am truly grateful to you for all this love and affection you are showering on me. I am really living these moments fully as I had dreamt for so many years.'

After a brief pause, Vikram said, 'Shall I tell you one thing Vineetha? You are a great lady. I admire your will power and attitude. Anyone in your place would have been in a state of depression. But the way you are coping with this, I have really no words of appreciation for you.'

Vineetha looked slightly puzzled. She said, 'Why what happened to me? I am alright . . .'

Vikram wondered for a moment whether she had forgotten that she was suffering from cancer and her chances of survival were only theoretical. He had told her about her illness in the hospital itself and they both had wept inconsolably then. Thereafter, she had never wept, though tears had rolled down Vikram's eyes several times after that when he was alone and thought about his and her fate.

Vikram said in a slightly practical way, 'Vineetha, you are not well. You are on medication. And you will get well soon. Right?'

Vineetha looked in his eyes and said in a firm voice, 'Vikram, I know that I am suffering from Liver Cancer and the chances of my survival are not very bright. That means I could die within the next 6 months. Right?'

Vikram was stunned to hear the plain truth spoken in such an emotionless manner from her. He said, 'Vineetha, that is what surprises me. You are coping up with this hard fact so well. Are you not afraid of death?' He wondered whether he should have asked such a question. But he could not conceal his inquisitiveness about her personality and attitude.

Vineetha smiled and said, 'Look Vikram, everyone who comes on this earth has to go one day. The day you are born, your day of departure is also decided. No one on this earth is immortal. Everyone goes as per his or her time. I am going a bit early, that's all. Why should there be any regrets for that? Why should I spoil my remaining little life worrying about my death when I am still alive? I have two choices in front of me today. Either I be happy or unhappy. I choose to be happy. And I say this because my being happy or unhappy is not going to change the outcome.'

Vikram was absolutely shocked to hear such high level philosophy from her. He had never expected this kind of wisdom from her. He had given several lectures across the world about life, death, duty, rewards, etc. But the truth had never hit him so hard before.

Vineetha continued, 'Vikram sir, I have learnt all this from you and your treasure of books.' She pointed at the shelves with books neatly arranged in them. 'While you were travelling around, I was reading all these books for time pass. I never knew that I would be so enlightened by them. I have realized that it does not matter 'how long' you live. What matters is 'how' you live . . . !'

It was Vikram's turn today to be a student and hear the lecture from Vineetha. The most practical and philosophical lecture containing the essence of all Vedas in them.

Vineetha said, 'Vikram, I have no desires left in life. I am ready to die any moment now. My time here is over. I was so lucky to have you as my husband, who cares for me so much. If at all God asks me again for the choice of my life partner in my next janma, I would request him for you.'

Vikram's eyes were filled up with tears. A huge lump filled his throat. His mind was going numb. He could not speak a single word.

Vineetha said, 'Oh yes, see how selfish I am. I did not think of you. I am not sure whether you would be happy with me. I am sorry I am leaving you alone halfway through. It is not my choice you know. God has kept the decisions on certain criteria with him otherwise people would stop respecting him. And Cancer is one of them. No one knows why it happens? There is still no definite cure as well. So, it is a game of lottery played by God. If the chit of your name comes, you have to go. No appeals and demands.'

Vikram could not take it anymore. He just closed her mouth with his palm and hugged her. They sat silently weeping for almost half an hour.

Today she was his guru. He learnt the meaning of life from a person who was about to die soon.

*   *   *

The producer friend of Rohit Khanna had given consent to cast Aniket as hero in his film after three auditions in his studio and giving Aniket a crash course in acting in his institute for 15 days. It was the happiest day in the life of Aniket. His long cherished dream was now about to get fulfilled. He had already taken an annual membership of a Gym and started doing extensive workouts under the guidance of a professional trainer. He was serious about his job. He could not have changed his face or his height, but by doing a regular exercise, he could definitely look much stronger and in masculine shape. This would add up to his screen presence and may also cover up the shortfalls in his acting skills, if any.

Somehow, Amit also started getting interested in this project of Aniket and took it seriously and positively. He was encouraging Aniket from time to time stating that there is no substitute for hard work in life, whichever field he chooses. A father's love for his son was evident as the skepticism and pessimism gave way for optimism and positive thinking.

Aniket was handed over a file containing the story of the film. It was a usual commercial film in which a hero, from a poor background falls in love with a rich man's daughter. It had all the ingredients of a masala movie, with 6 songs, fighting sequences, some emotions and the climax fight in a goods train carrying wild animals and reptiles.

The heroine's role was played by Reshma, an actor working in Bollywood for 4 years now. Her earlier films had done good business and she had also worked with two big actors before. That was a plus point for the film. There are people who go for films for different reasons. Some go for the hero, some for heroine, some for the songs and music, some for action. So, she would surely get her fans to see the film.

Initially Aniket felt very shy to act in scenes with her. He realized that acting was much more difficult than what he had thought before. The dialogue delivery was a tough job, as the actor had to modulate his tone according to the scene, the volume also had to be regulated, the expressions need to match the emotions expected from the scene, and the timing of dialogue delivery also had to be perfect. It was a tall order for a newcomer like Aniket.

Particularly in the scenes involving extreme emotions like loud laughter and crying he realized that he needed to learn the skills further. For the first time he also noticed, that it is much easier to cry than to laugh artificially. He realized how he used to criticize the actors while watching films, if the acting was not done well. And he felt tense that now he too would be judged by all the viewers for his acting skills.

Aniket was very punctual at the shootings. After two weeks of shooting, the unit realized that Aniket was a disciplined actor and was very serious about his work. He tried to read the script over and over again before the shot and also made rehearsals to get it right. He had some difficulty in dance steps, but with the help of the choreographer, he learnt it quickly. He was surprised to see that there was a big difference in what people see on the screen and the way shooting is done. For example, for a scene involving a fall from a height in the waterfalls, there was very little activity near the waterfalls. Most of the shooting was done in the studio in the backdrop of a white screen and the background was added later by the cinematographer. And while jumping from heights, there were enough protections like safety belts tied to strong ropes and heaps of cushions kept on ground to take care in case of any accidents. And added to that, most of the risky shots were done by a body double, a person with similar physique wearing same dress but shot from behind or a distance to cover the face. Aniket wondered that the hero in a film is not a hero in real life and also not even while shooting. It is all a make believe stuff deceiving the common man's senses.

After spending few days on the sets, Aniket started feeling very sorry for the extras working in the films. The extras were the actors who were used in dancing sequences, crowd scenes like market, railway stations etc. While rehearsing for the dance sequence, they would learn the steps very quickly and danced very well in the final shot. Aniket was sometimes embarrassed that while all the attention was on him by the producer and the director of the film while shooting, these extra actors were totally uncared for. They were paid paltry sums as compensation. What also pained him was that many of them were having too many personal problems on their domestic front, yet they kept a cheerful face on the camera and danced as if they were enjoying every moment of life. At times he overheard while they discussed among themselves during shooting breaks, and he was sad that their issues ranged from being unable to pay the rent to sending money home. Many of them had run away from homes in search of a dream which lay shattered. They all had landed in Mumbai aiming to make it big in Bollywood. But after waiting for the big break, which never came their way, they gradually lost their patience, self-confidence and money to survive. Then, one day they made big compromise of their lives to accept the roles of extras knowing very well, that once they get branded as extra actor, they would block all their chances of becoming hero or heroine forever. The difficult circumstances in life often make a person do many things which he never plans or wishes to do.

Aniket was reminded about a story in which a person, depressed with life, goes to meet a psychiatrist. He tells the psychiatrist that he was fed up with life and found no meaning in living further. He wanted to die. The psychiatrist advises him to go to the circus, which was playing in the town. The psychiatrist says that by watching the clown doing so many funny things in the circus, he would feel entertained and may feel refreshed from the depressing thoughts. But the psychiatrist is shocked when the person says that he was the same person working as clown in the circus. Sometimes, we perceive a person to be very happy, while he is actually not so happy in reality. According to one study, in today's world, more people are unhappy because of 'assumed happiness' of others, rather than their own problems.

And he felt it a bit ironical about Bollywood. Here, people with several personal problems acted as if they were extremely happy and thousands of people came to watch them on screen to momentarily forget their problems. No doubt, watching movies was considered an addiction in olden days. People used to forget their real miseries of life by watching for three hours the artificial happiness displayed by some actors.

After nearly six months of shooting, the film was almost ready. The publicity department was discussing on the advertisement through posters, on television, radio etc. Aniket was excited about the release of his first Bollywood film. He did not know whether it would be a success or a flop. Being a newcomer in the industry, he had no rights in the post production editing and scene finalization. However, he was invited to such meetings and he gave his opinion in right spirit wherever he felt like.

One day, Aniket was discussing the marketing strategies of the film with Niraj, the producer of his movie. Niraj got a phone call, which he picked up immediately. Throughout the conversation, Niraj appeared a bit tense and appeared to be bargaining something with the caller. Aniket was surprised, as to who this caller would be. After the call was over, Niraj took out his handkerchief and wiped the sweat from his face. He looked worried.

Aniket asked, 'Sir, what happened, any problem?'

Niraj did not say anything. He was thinking something deep inside.

Aniket persisted, 'Sir, please tell me . . . anything wrong?'

Niraj looked at Aniket and said, 'It was a call from a bhai. He wants to give me protection.'

Aniket was confused. He said, 'Did you ask for it?'

Niraj said, 'Aniket, you are too innocent for this field. There is a dark side to this industry, which no one really knows fully. The bhai wants to give me protection at a price. He wants money for that protection . . . he wants Rupees Five Crores. He says the music videos are selling very fast and we are making good money out of it.'

Aniket was stunned. He had heard about the underworld gangs, but never had dealt with any of them.

Niraj continued, 'When he says he will protect me, it means that no other bhai would ask for any money. That is called protection money.'

Aniket said, 'And what happens if we refuse to pay?'

Niraj looked coldly at Aniket and said, 'Remember what happened to Gulshan Kumar and Rakesh Roshan? These bhais sometimes take this extreme step to spread awareness among the Bollywood fraternity about the consequences of disobedience. They also keep a track on the movement of every star. If you are a star in demand, you would be under their radar.'

Aniket was shocked to listen to all this. This was something he had never imagined.

Niraj continued, 'Bollywood has become a big business. It is no more a gentleman's industry. The underworld money is regularly invested in the movies. Sometimes, movies are made just as an investment option for a bhai. The entire cast and crew is threatened to postpone all other schedules to create a commercially viable film at a certain cost and get double profit within six months of its release.'

Aniket was disturbed to find that he was so close to the underworld gangs without being aware of their presence. He was seeing a new price being paid for the stardom. That night he had an unusual fear when he went to sleep.

Finally the day came when the film was ready to be released all over India. The posters were up in all cities from one week. Whenever he spotted his posters on the streets of Mumbai while travelling in his car, he would see them with lot of appreciation and admiration and look at it till it went past. The driver could understand his excitement. At times, he wanted to stand in front of these posters in invisible form and look at the expressions on the faces of people watching these posters while passing by.

He had not slept the whole of the previous night thinking about the response his film would get at the box office. He was now able to imagine how the established stars would feel on the day of the release of their new films. It was a very anxious feeling. It was almost like the day of announcement of degree exam results for a studious student. His future depended on this day to a large extent. He had known some actors who became stars overnight after the release of their first film. Would he also be a lucky one to belong to that category? Would he be a flop hero? Would he get noticed by the audience as a promising hero? Would the journalists rate him positively or dismiss him? Suddenly he was overwhelmed with these thoughts.

The premier show was attended by several who's who in the Bollywood fraternity. Aniket was seeing so many stars together for the first time. And to be the centre of attraction among such a crowd was a great feeling. There were invitees from Amit's business contacts as well. The special invitees were Srikant, Vikram and Pankaj. However, Pankaj could not make it, due to his prior commitment of managing the annual temple festival in

Shantinagar on the same day. Amit had personally called them and invited them for this momentous day in his son's career.

Amit warmly welcomed them at the theatre. He was very happy that his son's hard work for last few months in this unconventional venture was now ready to bear fruits. For a moment he had forgotten that he had resisted his son from joining this field. Amit, Vikram and Srikant were standing together and discussing about their past and present. Amit was in a very happy mood to meet his old friends on this occasion of his son's achievement. They all remembered Pankaj as well. After the premier show was over, everyone congratulated Aniket for his good performance in the film.

And the first show of his film began screening at the theatres across India at around 12 noon on Friday, the timing for morning shows. Amit and Aniket performed a small pooja in their house praying to God to make the first film of Aniket a success.

Only God knew at that time whether Aniket would become a superstar or not.

*   *   *

Pankaj was now a hero not only in Shantinagar, but his popularity had spread to neighboring villages also. He was identified by the people as one who had social welfare as his prime agenda. He was recognized as the man, who genuinely wanted society to develop through more educated people, by inculcating moral ethics among the people and by making them self sustained. His passion for conserving the natural resources also appealed to the people.

One day, there were posters being stuck up on walls of Shantinagar about a political rally being organized in the village keeping in view the upcoming assembly elections. Many prominent leaders of the Jansatta party were expected to attend the rally. While he saw the posters, he spotted one familiar face. Yes, it was Srikant Joglekar. Pankaj had known that he had joined politics but had lost contact with him in last 5-6 years. Pankaj was surprised that Srikant had made so much progress during this period that his photos were being used on party posters as star attraction for the rally. He was very happy at the prospect of meeting his old friend after so many years.

The local people from the Jansatta party decided upon the seating arrangement on stage along with the Panchayat. From Shantinagar, Vasudev Rao and Pankaj were to be seated on the stage. And there were 4 speakers from the Jansatta party.

Pankaj had told his wife about Srikant's visit to Shantinagar and also hinted her that, if possible, he would also invite Srikant to his house for a dinner after the rally was over. She was happy to see Pankaj's enthusiasm for meeting his old friend and started making plans as to what could be the menu for the 'high profile' dinner. She was also looking forward to meeting her husband's childhood friend.

The day came when the rally was organized and there was a flurry of activities in Shantinagar. The access road was already repaired temporarily from the highway till the venue. It was temporarily repaired, as no one bothered about the condition of the road after the rally was over. People were used to these things and expected only so much from the government. However, no one really knew how much amount was sanctioned and paid off for the road repairs, as there was every possibility that much more amount was actually sanctioned for this purpose.

There were stalls set up near the venue for selling Samosa, Kachori, Cold drinks, Tea, Beedi etc. These were the regularly sold items in villages and such occasions presented the vendors with a sure market. These vendors did not have any political opinion and they were too happy whenever any party organized a rally there, as they could do a business worth 50 days on one day alone.

The rally was at 5 pm. The people started gathering there from 3 pm itself. There were many trucks and tractors parked beside the venue. It was a routine phenomenon to see the people being carted from nearby villages to attend the rally in trucks and tractors. These people would be given some snacks and some money at the end of the event. From the crowd gathered, it was difficult to predict, how many were carted and how many had come on their own accord. Nevertheless, it was quite obvious that whoever came themselves, had gathered there to see some excitement and have fun rather than hear the ideology from the party leaders. These were mainly people with no significant work and had lot of spare time to do anything else more worthwhile.

At 5.15 pm, suddenly there was a movement on ground as people got the news that the cavalcade had arrived. People stretched their necks to see in all directions whether they could catch a glimpse of the leaders. And soon, a fleet of cars came from a distance raising a storm of dust as it rolled. There were 7 ambassador cars followed and preceded by a police van. The cavalcade stopped right beside the stage and the leaders stepped out. There was a red carpet leading them to the stage. The local leaders rushed forward to receive the big politicians. It was considered an absolute necessity by all the active local party men that they should be seen in front receiving the guests to prove their loyalty to the party and the leaders. Sarpanch Vasudev Rao and Pankaj stood on the stage.

There were slogans raised 'Jansatta Party Zindabad' and 'Srikant Joglekar Zindabad'. Pankaj was overwhelmed to see his childhood friend receiving such a rousing reception by the party workers. He wondered how this guy had risen up the ladders of political success over all these years. Srikant was waving to the crowd in a characteristic leader style accepting the garlands as he moved forward through the crowd of supporters.

As Srikant reached the dais, he looked at Vasudev Rao and Pankaj. Srikant did not instantly recognize Pankaj. Pankaj was looking at him with a smile on his face. After a moment Srikant recognized Pankaj and both hugged each other on stage with a genuine smile on their faces. Some people who were attentive enough noticed that while Vasudev Rao had just greeted Srikant with a Namaste done with folded hands followed by a handshake, Pankaj had carried on the conversation after initial greetings as if he knew him very well.

Srikant was surprised to see Pankaj on the dais. He said, 'Pankaj, How are you? After a long time . . . ! How come you are here?'

Pankaj and Srikant sat on adjacent chairs on the stage. The local minions were giving away spirited speeches, which gave an excellent opportunity for Srikant and Pankaj to chat. Srikant noticed that all the local leaders heaped praise on Pankaj. He wondered what Pankaj had done for all these people that they were praising him so much . . . !

Srikant's turn came to deliver his speech and he rose amidst applause from the entire crowd. He spoke in a typical fashion about how his party was determined to focus on development and growth of the region. He elaborated on the various schemes undertaken by the government for welfare of poor people in the country, state and the region. He assured them of a better future if they voted a Jansatta party candidate to power in the next elections. He even mentioned about the scheme under which there were discussions with a US environmental agency to set up projects across India. He said, he would recommend one such plant in Shantinagar as well for the benefit of the people.

After the speech was over, Pankaj invited Srikant to his house for a dinner. He said, 'Srikant, we met after so many years. Let us talk today at length and revisit our past for some time.'

Srikant did not have any special agenda after this meeting and Pankaj was his good friend from childhood, so he couldn't say no to him. Srikant informed the other leaders about his plan and asked all of them to leave, leaving just two cars and a police van for him.

They went to Pankaj's house and sat on the plastic chairs laid out neatly in the lawn cum garden in front of the house, cultivated so beautifully by Pankaj over the years. Srikant was happy to see that Pankaj lived in such natural environment. For a moment, he envied Pankaj. The neighbors were crowding outside Pankaj's house to see the minister but were controlled by the police. None of them knew that actually it was not a minister meeting a respected personality of Shantinagar, but it was a re-union of two old friends.

Srikant said, sipping tea which had a rustic flavor, 'Pankaj, I am truly happy and also surprised to see you after so many years. And what is this? You look so young still . . . ! How do you manage to keep fit and look so energetic?'

Pankaj replied with modesty, 'Nothing much. I just take care of my health a bit more than what others do. I do regular exercises, Yoga, diet control, drinking lots of water etc. That keeps me fit and the natural surrounding with clean and fresh air do their bit in adding to my efforts.'

Srikant felt somewhat guilty that he did nothing of these. His daily schedules made him have irregular lunches, mostly rich in calories. He did not do any regular exercise. He did not even walk a few steps for exercise every day.

Naturally, he was having a roundish figure with a plump face.

He quickly changed the topic on health to avoid further embarrassment for not doing anything to protect his health the 'Pankaj way'.

Srikant said, 'Oh that is fantastic. And also it is good to see that you have earned a name for yourselves as I could see from the response and applause from the crowds while you spoke. How come you landed here in this village?'

Pankaj narrated to him the entire story about how he accidentally started taking tuitions, then how he opened his coaching centre, how he left the job and concentrated on the coaching classes, then the turning point of helping the society and shifting to Shantinagar and then his recent endeavors in the environmental field.

Srikant was listening intently. He was appreciating the thought process of Pankaj as he progressed in life. He developed a kind of respect for Pankaj that he had forsaken his personal pleasures for the benefit of the society and people around him. He wondered that how individual priorities define a person's lifestyle.

Pankaj asked Srikant, 'And Srikant, now tell me, how did you become such a big politician? I am thrilled to see the power you wield, with so many party workers around you, the police giving you protection wherever you go . . .'

Srikant smiled and said with pride, 'Pankaj it had been a long journey. I was jobless after graduation for some time. Then accidentally I participated in some rallies and was noticed. I joined a party, became a party worker, and became a corporater and then a MLA. And now I am a minister. An Environment minister . . . !'

And then, as if he remembered something, he said, 'Pankaj, you have built up such an excellent public support. Why don't you join politics? You will have a bright future . . .'

Pankaj was taken aback at this statement. He said somewhat impersonally, 'No Srikant, I can't join politics. What would I do by joining politics? I am very happy the way I am.'

Srikant said, 'No Pankaj, by joining politics you can serve people better. Look at me . . .'

Pankaj hesitated for a while as if deciding whether to say or not and then said, 'Srikant, I am able to serve people the way I am. I do not need an official position to help people. If you have real intention of helping people, you can do so irrespective of your position. Do you know that Gandhiji never held any position in the government? Yet he had so much power . . . and please don't mistake that I am comparing myself with Gandhiji or something like that. I just wanted to emphasize that if you have a sincere desire to serve people you don't need to have any official power!'

Srikant was a bit taken aback at this rather blunt remark. He said, 'Do you intend to say that we do nothing for the people? What is the difference between you and me? You also serve people and I also serve people, right?'

Pankaj smiled and said, 'There is a difference Srikant. I do it as my passion and philosophy, while you do it for power and money. You do not have real intentions of helping people. All your interests are only in helping yourselves. Can you show me one project you have sanctioned without accepting any money?'

Pankaj suddenly realized that he had spoken a bit too much. He tried to control himself from saying more.

Srikant looked sad at this unexpected development in the friendly discussions. He said, 'Pankaj, what you think is not 100% correct. You are alleging things which are not true.'

Pankaj tried to save the situation. He said, 'Sorry Srikant, if I have hurt your sentiments. But, please understand that when I said YOU, what I meant was the political class in this country. The politics today is filled with all such people who are interested only in their well being. They are corrupt people, who have no interest in common man's welfare. They have turned this politics into a business. It is like a business sector in which you spend money to get into power and then you make 5 times the money in 5 years. It is a pure plain business and nothing else. And these people spoil the entire political class.'

Srikant was somewhat relieved at this explanation of sorts from Pankaj. Otherwise it was appearing as a direct personal attack. He said, 'Yes Pankaj I agree with

you. There are many people around like what you have
described. The whole system is rotten, in a way.'

Pankaj said, 'Ok Srikant, you are a part of this system,
right? And you are in this for a long time now. What
efforts have you made to change the system? So long as
you are a part of the system, you will also be considered by
outsiders as one among them. Every drop of an ocean has
the same percentage of salt content as the rest of the ocean
has . . . And for that matter, I have to do some explanation
to the people of Shantinagar about our old friendship,
otherwise they would assume that by inviting you to my
home, I am nurturing some political ambitions, or trying
to cut a deal with you on the environmental project
you talked about in your speech. Thankfully, people
of Shantinagar do believe me so there is no problem as
such . . .'

This question stumped Srikant. He felt embarrassed that
his old friend was not very comfortable at meeting him
and would be required to explain about it to his people.
He did not expect such a direct remark from his friend.
And unfortunately he had no answer as well. He was
wondering in his mind what Pankaj thought about him.
While initially he had accused Srikant, later he said that
his comments were in general and not directed at him
personally.

To avoid this embarrassment, Pankaj said, 'I am extremely
sorry Srikant, I should not have taken this discussion this
far. Let us change the topic. Please forgive me, if I have
hurt your sentiments.'

Then they discussed about their other two friends. Srikant told him about his meeting with Amit sometime back. Pankaj was very happy to hear that Amit has become a big businessman. Srikant briefed him about their meeting in his office but censored the unpleasant part of their conversation. Srikant informed Pankaj that Vikram was a successful motivational speaker travelling around a lot giving training to the corporate houses. He also informed Pankaj about Amit's son Aniket, who had become a film star.

Srikant had a good dinner and left shortly thereafter. Pankaj thanked him once again for gracing his house and having dinner with him. Both were happy to have met after several years.

However, Srikant was in a deep introspection mode while he was travelling back.

CHAPTER 11

Vikram had a tough role to play these days. While he was pained to see Vineetha fighting cancer with a brave face, he had to appear cheerful just like her. Vineetha was not having any consistent pain or anything like that. She was on a regular medication and had some pain once in a while. But the remaining time, she was like a normal person.

He wanted to make these days memorable for her. She had limited time. Her time was running out. He was not sure whether the treatment would be successful or not. He was expecting the best while being prepared for the worst. And it was extremely difficult for him to even imagine the worst. She was a part of his life. Without her, he was incomplete. He desperately wanted her to continue to live.

One day he told Vineetha, 'Vinee, shall we go on a world tour? I want you to see the world, how beautiful it is . . .'

Vineetha replied in her usual mood, 'Oh Vicky, leave it. I know the world is beautiful. I had travelled a few countries before our marriage and have seen different parts of the world. And you know what? I like India very much. India is the best country in the world any day.'

Vikram was surprised to hear this.

He still said, 'Vinee, we can go anywhere in the world, just anywhere. We can see the Seven Wonders of the World. Or we can go to the beaches in Hawaii . . . we can visit the Egyptian Pyramids . . . we can go to Disneyland . . . We can climb up the Eifel tower . . .'

Vikram wanted to offer the best to her. He did not want her to have a regret later (which was coming a bit sooner.)

Vineetha composed herself and said, 'Vikram, there are many things in life you want to do. Can you do all of them? It is physically impossible. If you expect that you see the entire world and experience all the pleasures in this world in one life, it is humanly impossible. You just can't do it.'

Vikram sensed that she was about to start all over again with her wisdom.

Vineetha continued, 'Vikram, at least I am lucky that I know that I am going to die soon. Just think about all those who die in an accident. They don't even know that they are going to die. Their loved ones do not get a chance to express their feelings for them one last time. It happens in few seconds and the person is gone. Every person is destined for certain moments of life on this earth and he lives them. He can't live one moment less or one moment more.'

Vikram wondered how her thoughts had shaped ever since she was diagnosed with cancer. He questioned her, 'How do you call yourselves lucky Vineetha, when you are in such a condition?'

Vineetha said, 'Vikram, Yes, I am lucky because I am leaving this world while I am still young, I have experienced infinite happiness during my life time and because I am not a burden on anyone for a single day. You know Vikram, it is a real bad luck if I was bedridden with a paralysis and you had to look after me. I hate such a life. Instead of living 10 years like that, I would love to live only 10 minutes happily on my own.'

Vikram was learning the new definition of happiness and luck. He had no clue how to react on such occasions. He had been giving lectures on management and mythology all these years, but she was almost giving him the essence of it all in a very simple and easy language to understand.

Vikram asked her, 'Vineetha, do you think that everyone who dies in an accident is lucky?'

Vineetha said, 'Yes, of course. See they have no sufferings. All their sufferings are over in few seconds. It is the easiest death one should aspire for. No headaches, no bedridden dependencies, no medicines. Blessed are the ones who die an instant death.'

Vikram was stunned to hear the comments about death in such a casual manner.

Vineetha said, 'Yes, there is one thing though. We do not know God's schemes every time. Many times, we miscalculate the current occurrence because of our limited knowledge about the future.'

Vikram was intently listening. As usual, he had no words.

Vineetha said, 'Vikram, the world is full of unhappy people because they worry in the present about the future which is unknown and the past which they cannot correct. They just don't live in the present. And that is the reason of their unhappiness.

I live each and every moment as it comes. Just because I may not be there around after few weeks does not mean that I spend days and nights worrying about it. Instead, I appreciate the life in every breath I take. I appreciate the promising sunrise, the coolness of a gentle breeze, the poetic sunsets etc. It is sad that when I am not there, they will still be there, but one person less in this world, who appreciates their true value.'

'So, Vikram, where do you want to take me? Vineetha said, as if returning from a philosophical world to a more practical world.

Vikram asked, 'Tell me, where we shall go . . .'

Vineetha said, 'Vikram, India is a great country. I love my India. I would like to travel across India. Ideally, I would like to see each and every part of India, as it has a different flavor. Be it the Kaleidoscopic Kolkata, or Charming Chennai; Magnificent Mumbai or the Delightful Delhi. Look around the world and you will realize that India is the only country with so many diverse cultures, languages and habitats living as one family amicably for so many years. I would love to choose the best among these places and visit them before I . . .'

So, Vikram and Vineetha took out a map of India and started identifying which places they could afford to go. 'Afford' with respect to time and not money.

It is said that time is money. In their case, time was much more valuable than money . . .

*   *   *

Aniket was anxiously waiting for the results from trade pundits whether the new film was a success or not. By evening that day, the results started pouring in that the film was drawing reasonable crowds, if not packed houses. Aniket was having mixed feelings. He was happy that at least the film did not get a poor opening with empty halls while at the same time he did not have the honors of attracting the large audiences. The marketing had done their job well, by airing the promos on various television channels, radio channels and the routine ones like newspaper ads and hoardings across all major cities.

However, something strange happened on the second day. The collections in theatres were recorded slightly more than the opening day. And on the third day, which was a Sunday, the film ran to almost 95% packed theatres. Aniket was pleasantly surprised.

So, the most powerful method of publicity, the word of mouth publicity was working here for him. The people who saw the film were giving good reviews about the film, which propelled more people to the theatres. And by the second week, the film was declared a hit. The film had come as a refresher in the midst of routine films with similar storyline. The film had very good music, a neat storyline and the refreshing new face of a hero.

It is not exactly clear as to what will click in the film industry. It all depends on various factors like the movies released during the same period, the movies released during last one year and more importantly, the luck of the people involved in making the film. That is why, many times a low budget film becomes a hit while a multi starrer with all big names associated with it bites the dust. The producers have still not been able to figure out a formula for making a successful film. Every film is like a gamble. If it works it works, otherwise not.

It was Zanjeer, a film rejected by several superstars of that period which turned Amitabh Bachchan's fortunes overnight and made him a superstar who ruled Bollywood for several decades to come. It was a low budget 'Slumdog Millionaire' which got the honors of winning several coveted international awards. At the same time, there were several big budget films made by reputed film personalities which simply bombed at the box office. The notable among them were Mera Naam Joker by Raj Kapoor, Kaala Pathhar by Yash Chopra, and Trimurti by Subhash Ghai etc. So, it is a big mystery as to what will click in the Bollywood and what will not. It all depended on luck, finally.

Aniket was on cloud nine after the verdict of people. He was very happy and excited to read the reviews of the film in various newspapers and film magazines describing about how a star was born. He started moving around with an air of confidence. People started recognizing him wherever he went. They were jostling to get his autograph. He had to set up his office with a bodyguard, a secretary who will take all his phone calls and keep him informed about all his appointments. He had a driver now and tinted the glasses of his car so that people could not recognize him inside the car otherwise there would be traffic issues. He also started wearing dark goggles which was considered to be a sign of celebrity.

He started getting more offers from the other producers and directors who wanted to cash in on his stardom by making film as quickly as possible. The film industry is also a bit funny like share market, where often the emotions take precedence over the plain logic. He signed a record 6 films within next 4 months.

He was nominated for the award for 'best debutante actor—male' in almost all the award functions. It was a dream come true for Aniket to attend all these functions with his parents and make them proud by going up to the stage to receive the awards. In all his speeches, he thanked his parents for trusting him and encouraging him in his difficult times. Amit and his wife were equally proud to be treated in a special way at such functions by getting the front rows reserved for them.

Amit finally thought that he would have made a big mistake if he had not allowed his son to follow his passion of acting in movies. He thought that Aniket would not have been as successful in his family business. But his desire to hand over the reins of his business to his son would now remain unfulfilled.

Aniket had a world of his own now. He had many friends from Bollywood industry. He was being invited for many private parties of the Bollywood fraternity where he came in contact with several new faces, whom he had earlier seen only on screen or in magazines. He had become a public figure now. At times, when he stood in the balcony for a few minutes, a crowd would gather below watching him and waving hysterically at him. He used to graciously wave back and step back inside the house. He realized that he was slowly paying the price of being a celebrity. He could no longer walk outside his house freely, he could not go to his favorite hotels without being noticed, he could not spend some calm moments on beaches, and he could not go shopping at the usual places. He had to upgrade himself to places which were beyond the reach of ordinary people. And there he would meet only the high profile people who were having more money than decency. These people would look at other people and gauge who was richer among them. It was somewhat hypocritical but that was the norm and he had to follow the suit, as he had no options.

Aniket had become a superstar. His dream was fulfilled.

*   *   *

The delegation from US environmental agency was back in Srikant's office for further discussions on the subject of setting up the Effluent Treatment Plants all over India. In the meantime, Srikant had briefed the 'high command' about the proposal and obtained an approval to proceed with the project.

Srikant was involuntarily thinking about how much money he could make from this initiative. There had to be some commission in this for him and the distribution chain upwards in the power hierarchy. The money involved was big one and there were less chances of anyone resisting the acceptance/distribution of commission amounts, since the amounts were coming from governmental bodies and not some individuals. The risks were higher when individuals were involved in the deals.

Somehow, he was not very comfortable thinking about money. Since he met Amit few months back, he was not feeling good that he had asked for money from his old friend. But the past is past and cannot be reversed. Added to that, his meeting with Pankaj sometime ago further added in lowering his self esteem. He was surprised to hear the views about politicians in the common man's minds. Normally, no one spoke to him like that, as he was mostly surrounded by opportunistic politicians who only told him what pleased him and did not say the truth. Moreover, the definition of truth and goodness were quite different in the political circles and no one in this field ever wondered what the people thought about them. And those who thought did not bother about them. The system had become so insensitive that no one cared about the people who elect them to power term after term.

Srikant wondered what he would do after earning so much money. He had made lot of investments and bought enough property for him and his next seven generations to survive even if they did not earn a penny. So, why to earn more? He felt that he was becoming hypocritical. On one hand he was thinking of these 'pure thoughts' but his actions were not exactly matching with his ideas. Maybe that some day in future when these ideas take strong roots those ideas might compel him to control and alter his actions as well.

He began wondering what he would do if he stopped taking money from the people. In politics there were hardly any positions which were free from corruption. He suddenly realized that yes there were some positions where one can enjoy the power with dignity as well, which had relatively cleaner image than others. They were the assignments like being ambassadors to other countries, governors of states, members of planning commission etc. These positions had lesser powers yet they were dignified and appeared clean to the common man. Normally these positions were occupied by those senior politicians who were losing their clout and utility to the party because of the shifting power centers and their dwindling powers to win elections for the party. He decided in his mind that once this deal is through, he would start working towards one such position. He had reached a stage in his life where he had earned enough money and enjoyed power as well. Now he wanted to have a clear conscience. The urge for this new feeling started gaining ground in his mind after he had the game changing meetings with his old friends, Amit and then Pankaj.

Srikant asked his secretary to send the delegation inside his chamber. The trio came in immediately. They were interested in knowing the government stand on their proposal. This project would have given a big boost to the environmental protection initiatives across the globe. They settled on the meeting chairs with their bags placed on the side tables.

Srikant wished them a good morning and started the topic after exchanging the pleasantries. Srikant said, 'Mr. Khurana, I am happy to inform you that our government has approved in principle the proposal put forward by you. This means that we would be willing to go ahead with this, provided all the technicalities and commercial aspects are worked out. The proposal shall be submitted to our environmental committee who shall review it and give their advice.'

Mr. Khurana was very happy to hear this. He looked at his colleagues with happiness and looked back at Srikant. He said, 'Sir that is a real good news for us. We were the force behind this proposal for several months now and were hoping that it is implemented. This is the success of our efforts for all these months for this noble cause to protect the mother earth from further degeneration.'

Srikant nodded in approval. He was thinking in his mind about the commercial part now. It was the right time to discuss this. He cleared his throat and said, 'Mr. Khurana, what is your outlay for this project for the facilitation charges? I mean the reports have to be right for us to proceed forward. And the positive review reports generally come with a cost.'

Srikant paused to look at Khurana's expressions. He wanted to see Khurana's reactions and see whether he was comfortable in talking about the commercial terms in presence of his colleagues.

Khurana smiled and said, 'Of course, sir. We have a standard of 10% of the approved project cost as facilitation cum recommendation charges. We shall deposit this amount in whichever bank account across the world as you desire. As per our initial estimates, the Indian government share comes to Rs. 700 Crores, so we are talking of about Rs. 70 Crores as the facilitation charges.'

There was a pause for a while. The cards from both sides were in the open now. The atmosphere had become a bit lighter, as the things were now getting into minor details of implementation.

And suddenly, as if he was waiting for this moment, Mr. Khurana took out one of the bags and opened it on the table facing Srikant. He said, 'Sir, here is the token advance of Rs. 50 Lakhs. The bag could carry only this much without appearing suspicious in any manner.'

Srikant looked at the crisp notes of Rs. 1000 stacked neatly in bundles of 100 each. He quickly calculated the total and it appeared to be the said amount. It was not professional ethics to count the notes in such transactions and especially not in such big deals. Trust was the factor.

Srikant smiled and took the bag. He closed it and kept it beside his chair. They stood up to shake hands and decided to meet after around two weeks to take this further. Srikant saw them till the office door. It was his custom that he accompanied all important people till the door while they were leaving, as a matter of courtesy.

He came back to his chair and asked his secretary for a cup of tea. He was thinking deeply in his mind about the money. He was not happy, as he used to be always. The frequent thoughts about being honest were making him uncomfortable. He somehow convinced his mind that this was his last deal and he would push for a position, which did not encourage any corruption. He wanted to lead an honest life.

That night, while he was about to sleep at about 11 pm, his mobile phone rang. It was the leader of opposition in Lok Sabha, Deen dayal Asthana. He wondered what Deen Dayal had to do with him at such an hour. And moreover, he did not share a good rapport with him inside and outside the parliament. During the last term, as leader of opposition, Srikant had put Deen Dayal in serious embarrassment over his inefficient handling of his department by exposing his blunders.

Srikant said, 'Hello, Deen Dayal ji, how are you? Any problem?'

Deen Dayal said, 'Srikant ji, Namashkar. How much are you willing to pay for your reputation?'

Srikant did not quite understand. He just said, 'What?'

Deen Dayal said, 'Srikant ji, you can't make Rs. 70 Crores just like that. You have already taken the advance of Rs. 50 Lakhs, right?'

Srikant was dumbfounded. He did not know what to say. He just held on to the phone listening to his loud heartbeat.

Deen Dayal said, 'What happened Srikant ji? Bolti band ho gayi? The cost of your reputation is Rs. 25 Crores. Otherwise tomorrow evening prime time news shall carry the sting operation videos on every news channel. Remember the bags carried by Mr. Khurana and his team members? The hidden cameras have recorded every word and every expression of your conversation.'

Srikant could not believe his ears. The whole environmental project was a sting operation carried out at the behest of Deen Dayal. He was on camera accepting the money and promising them the sanction at a cost.

Deen Dayal continued, 'Srikant ji, I can understand how you feel. Anyway, you have time till tomorrow evening 6 pm. If I do not hear from you, then please do watch all the news channels at 9 pm for the detailed coverage of this mega scandal. Good night . . . !'

Srikant heard the phone go dead on the other side. He was holding the phone for several seconds after it was disconnected. His mind was going numb and his body was lightly shaking. His throat was going dry. He could not think anything.

He had 19 hours to decide . . . !

CHAPTER 12

Vikram and Vineetha had visited the doctor in the morning. The doctor slightly altered the prescription as if experimenting something new as the old combination of medicines was not working out as expected. He was uttering all optimistic words like 'you will get well soon', 'good improvement' etc but both of them could secretly see his gloomy thoughts behind his artificial pleasant expressions. Somehow they started feeling that they had limited time now.

They were not very happy while returning from the hospital. They again started thinking about their site seeing trip, which was expected to act like an attention diverter and bring them some temporary cheer. Sometimes a change of place, though only for a few days, does bring some respite from the ongoing problems in life.

Vikram asked Vineetha, 'So, where are we going?'

Vineetha said, 'Let us do one thing. I don't think there is enough time for us to see everything that I want to . . .'

Vikram felt helpless. How he wished he could borrow some time from the creator so that they could travel as they desired.

Vineetha continued, 'Let us go to one pilgrimage place, one beach other than Mumbai and a hill station . . . no let us make the hill station in summer . . ."

She stopped abruptly as she realized that she may not live till the next summer. How a person's thought process sometimes takes for granted the routine things, which no longer remain routine in exceptional circumstances like the one they were facing.

She added hastily, 'No need for a hill station. Let us just go to a pilgrimage and a serene beach.'

Finally they decided to go to Mathura Vrindavan for pilgrimage and Kerala for the beaches.

They packed their baggage and set off for their last journey together. Vikram had booked the best hotels for them in both these places.

He found her cheerful as always during the journey. She was looking at everything around her and enjoying it. For example, she enjoyed the flying birds and wondered what objectives they had in their lives. She looked at the tall trees and felt pity that they were bound to one place lifelong without as much even able to show their expression of gratitude to the person who watered it when it was a small sapling. She looked at the white clouds moving in the blue sky and wondered from where they came and where they were heading to. Did they have emotions? She wondered about the children playing around and felt that children represented life on earth. They were so innocent, so full of enthusiasm, so noble as to forget and forgive others while playing . . . they were much matured than men in this aspect.

On Vineetha's request, they had travelled in trains as she wanted to enjoy the journey. She believed that the journey is as important as reaching the destination. Many times in life, we have so much excitement for reaching the destination that we miss enjoying the journey. And all the destinations may not be as exciting as we had imagined. After all, life is also one long journey which every one of us starts with our birth and ends with our death. We get different co-passengers at different stages of life. If in this journey, we keep travelling blindly waiting for the destination, the entire life time would be simply wasted.

The definition of pleasure changes as we progress in our lives. One must learn to experience the joy of jumping around and playing around in parks with friends as a child. One should enjoy studying hard in the defining years of life for shaping ones career. The pleasures of getting married and watching the children grow is something exquisite and should not be missed. The pleasures, when children come home from school flashing their good mark sheets, are precious. The sense of pride on achievements of one's children is too valuable. And finally, the pleasure obtained to play with the grandchildren has no equivalent in this world. In life, one needs to enjoy these simple moments. Often people wait for something big to happen so that they can enjoy. They are sadly mistaken for the life's pleasures are almost always found in smaller moments. And in search for the big moments, people lose the happiness hidden even in the small moments of life.

While travelling in train, her attention was caught by a person in the next aisle who refused to exchange his lower berth to help an old lady who had an upper berth. He was constantly saying that he had reserved the berth two months ago and had the right to travel on the same berth. The old lady's family was urging him and requesting him to occupy the higher berth, but he was obstinately refusing the proposal.

Vineetha was wondering at the nature of this person. Here she was not sure how long she would live and was preparing to leave this world once for all, while this person was trying to hold on to his reserved berth for a journey of just few hours. What a contrast . . . !

In the temples of Mathura and Vrindavan, she prayed with same devotion as she had done earlier. She was not angry at God for his act of deciding to invite her to his abode much before she would have liked to. Her faith in God did not seem to have waned. Vikram wondered what she asked God now. Did she ask for extension on earth?

While eating the Prasad on the steps of the temple, Vikram could not resist himself and asked her, 'What did you ask God, Vineetha?'

Vineetha looked in his eyes and said, 'Vikram, from the beginning I never asked anything to God. He knows what is best for me. I should not influence his mind in granting me a favor which may not be good for me in the long run. We are too short sighted to know the implications of his wishes. He grants us his blessings according to what we deserve. He never gives anyone anything less or more. Everyone on this earth comes with a zero balance. The more we do right things, more blessings we get.'

Vikram was again stunned to hear this plain philosophy from her.

Vineetha said, 'That is why, sometimes we do not know his blessings. We tend to always think those things to be good for us, which we desire for. It is not always true. For example, I did not ask for a long life by even one day, you know. It will be good for me when he decided that I should die. If I pray to him to make me live longer, and he makes me live longer indeed, but lying paralyzed on bed what good it would do to me or you? That would in fact be more painful.'

Vikram appreciated her enlightened thoughts and the balanced thinking process amidst such personal crisis also. He changed the topic as he could no more listen to her blunt thoughts, which she spoke as if describing a lesson from a third standard textbook.

They went to Kerala and stayed on a houseboat. The serenity and calmness of the place appeared to give her lot of happiness, as she was living every moment. She used to look at the silent yet powerful backwaters, appreciate the trees lined along the beach, and feel the cool breeze touching her face. While on beach, she went into knee deep waters and felt the tides hitting her feet every 10 seconds. Intermittently a big tide used to come roaring wetting her legs a few inches higher. She looked at the sand moving with the water into the sea for some distance and waiting for the next tide to take it further. There was serenity she was looking for in the entire scene. She enjoyed herself.

Her last wish of visiting a pilgrimage place and a beach was fulfilled. Now she was ready for the 'future' . . . !

*   *   *

Pankaj and his wife were preparing to go to the United States of America for a short period. Their only son, Rahul had decided to settle there. After pursuing his higher studies there, he had got a good job immediately thereafter. Pankaj did not force his son, Rahul to come back to India, as he believed in letting the mature adults take their own decisions concerning their lives. He advised people on various matters, but never forced anyone to follow his advice. He felt that everyone had a right to think independently and take the decisions best suited to the circumstances. His philosophy was that everyone has a different angle of viewing at the things and everyone must respect other's opinion.

Initially, when his son was preparing to go to US, he was deeply hurt inside his heart. He felt that his son was not following his footsteps of devoting himself for the welfare of mother India. But then, he had series of discussions with Rahul on the subject and finally yielded to his wishes. Rahul was of the opinion that the world had considerably shrunk now compared to previous generation and it did not really matter whether one worked in India or America. The different economies in the world were lot more interdependent today than they were ever before. One of the drawbacks of the uncontrollable globalization is that the day American markets crash for any reason whatsoever, next day markets across the world would also dip, irrespective of some handsome results declared by some native giant companies in different countries. And the day American markets rose, the trend would be blindly followed by all countries without a reason.

It was not that Rahul was not patriotic, but his definition of serving the country was slightly different from that of his father. In USA, whenever the national anthem was played on Indian functions, his heart would swell with pride by looking at the Indian flag. And on Independence Day functions when they played the patriotic songs, his eyes would be filled with tears. His wife, Aruna, however, did not have the same intensity of feelings, as she was brought up there. Her father had settled there since a long time.

The occasion for Pankaj and his wife to visit USA was the same which forces many Indian old couples to visit USA . . . for helping their children in managing the new arrival in their family. They had planned to stay there for 4 months. One month before the delivery and three months afterword. Pankaj was not very excited about visiting a foreign country as his wife was. She was preparing for this visit since few weeks and was equally thrilled about the occasion for which they were going there. It is a momentous occasion for any person to become a grandparent. It has also been observed that people have a tendency to love their grandchildren more than their own children. Probably it has something to do with their own profile at these two different times. When a person's children are growing up, he has his own priorities in life while in case of grand children most people lead a retired life, and the only priority in life is to enjoy the life in its small moments.

As the plane landed in New York airport, Pankaj and his wife were thrilled to step for the first time on a foreign land. Rahul had come to the airport to pick them up. The first thing Pankaj noticed on arrival in the USA was the cleanliness at the airport and the good interiors with proper signages everywhere. Rahul had a big posh car and he was very delighted to receive his parents and drive them in his car. Pankaj could not hide the expressions of his appreciation for his son's achievements. The roads were also neat with proper markings and without any potholes. He wondered why such roads could not be constructed and maintained in India. By pure logic, if something was possible in USA, it should be possible in India too. But then he remembered the obvious reasons why it does not happen . . . a large portion of the amount meant for the construction and maintenance of roads is not spent on the right cause. It goes somewhere else. For a fraction of second, he suddenly remembered Srikant and for the first time, hated him.

Aruna received her in-laws very well and had prepared a delicious lunch for them by taking much effort in spite of her delicate condition. Pankaj's wife was extremely happy to see that their daughter-in-law had accorded them a best welcome they could think of. After lunch they had a good nap to fight the jet lag, which was going to trouble them for the next few days.

*   *   *

Aniket's next two films bombed at the box office. He was disappointed with life. He was experiencing a feeling which he never experienced before. It was a feeling of rejection. And that too, at such a large scale . . . ! It was then that he realized the tremendous pressure in which the Bollywood stars live. During the release of every new movie, they have to just surrender themselves in front of the audience hoping for their favorable reviews and response.

Life is no more same in the moments of failure. The same life which appeared very rosy and beautiful started looking scary and unpredictable to Aniket. He started losing his confidence. He did not know what to do. Was he really bad? Was the success of his first film a fluke? These thoughts started occupying his mind most of the time.

He had read various stories about how the other stars had taken defeat in their careers. Some had taken to drinking. Some became reclusive to the extent that they were not seen anywhere in social circles. And some had become even abusive with those around them. It was the first time he realized that stardom comes with a price. This was a new price experienced by him—the price of anxiety to retain and regain the stardom. Every star was under a pressure every moment to ensure that he does not slip in the popularity charts. The task was much more difficult for the female stars who needed to look attractive and maintain the strict diets even though no shooting schedule was on for a few weeks.

Amit was always by his side even in his failures. He used to always motivate and encourage Aniket saying that success and failure were but a part of the game. Amit advised him that failure was only when a person gives up trying. In fact failures to some extent are sometimes very helpful in shaping ones personality, character and attitudes. Success is more likely to spoil a person in hundred ways but failure teaches him hundred things. A failure makes a person humble in his dealing with others. He starts believing that his efforts do not always determine the results. There are some other elements too like God's willingness, luck, blessings of the elders etc which play a crucial supporting role in achieving success.

A failure makes a person to look up to other's achievements in a positive light. A failure gives a person an excellent opportunity to evaluate his skill set and the necessary changes required in them to convert the failure into a success. The times keep changing. And the skills required to be successful are very different in different times. For example, Don Bradman, hailed as the super star of cricket would probably have been a failure in modern version of T20 cricket. Because his skill set was that of a tenacious player who played long innings consistently in test cricket. Similarly, the degree of success of Amitabh Bachchan and Dhirubhai Ambani would have been different in their respective fields if they were born twenty years before or after their actual dates, because the players in the game were different, the rules were different, the opportunities were different and it is not guaranteed that they would have clicked in those conditions. They might have been more successful or less successful.

Aniket started observing a change in the way other actors and even his co stars treated him in public functions. They did not give him the importance which he got after the success of his first film. They were not keen in getting photographed with him by the media. They just greeted him and exchanged pleasantries while continuing to be in their own circles. This pained him. He felt that the entire industry was a big hypocrite. It was a place where human relations were not given much importance. What was only valued was the 'salability' of a star. If you are salable, you are a big star. Otherwise no one will look at you. The same people in industry who used to flock around him in his successful days were now avoiding him.

He wondered how these people in film fraternity would react when they will gradually become old. Unfortunately, no one will remain young forever. With every passing moment, one is getting older and older. How will these stars feel when at the age of say fifty or sixty when they will no more be able to play the roles of a hero? It would be very difficult for the people who have basked in popularity for several years to go unnoticed on streets. Their heart would cry out loud to see that they are no more revered or even recognized by the same people who made them heroes one day. Rajesh Khanna was one such personality whose three years of superstardom became a curse when he struggled for success for rest of his life and lived for 40 years in this condition.

Just two flops gave Aniket the wisdom which even ten hits would not have given. He had learnt that he needed to rise in life whenever he fell down. He learnt that there would be moments in everyone's life when one feels down and out. Those are the moments when one needs to relook at his capabilities, skills and reinvent himself. Success and failure are both transient in nature. They come and go. They may not always reflect the true potential of a person.

The true character of a person is revealed not by the way one behaved in his successful times. It is reflected by the way he carried himself in his failures.

It was during these tough times that Aniket got closer to Reshma, his heroine of first film. She had one more hit film after working with Aniket and of course was doing very well. He confided in her about his feelings and expressed how miserable he felt with these two back to back flops. She consoled him and motivated him by saying that success and failure are but two sides of a coin. Many times, we do not value success unless we taste failure as well. Unless there is a bright sunshine, we do not value the cool shade. Unless we take pains to drive the bicycle up slope, we do not experience the pleasure in riding down the slope without pedaling.

One day, when she appeared a bit out of mood, he asked her what was the issue. Reshma at first did not say anything, but then said something which shocked Aniket.

Reshma said, 'Aniket, I am getting too stressed out with my busy shooting schedules. I need rest. I am working three shifts every day. I fly to different cities and get to work within two hours of reaching there. I am not getting a proper sleep of minimum 6 hours also. It has been few weeks since I had a deep sleep and woke up without an alarm leisurely.'

Aniket was stunned to hear her personal issues which he never expected.

Reshma continued, 'I need rest Aniket. I want to spend some time alone . . .'

Aniket said, 'So what is the problem Reshma? Cancel your shooting schedules for one month and go for a holiday to a hill station like Ooty or Shimla.'

Reshma said not looking at him, 'That is the problem. My family is using me as a money making machine. My father wants me not to skip any of my schedules so that the payments come in time and he can invest that money in his business. He doesn't care whether I am enjoying my work or even whether I am keeping good health or not. He doesn't care to even ask me how I am coping up with my busy schedules. He just wants me to sign as many assignments as possible. Normally I would have loved to be in a situation, where I am fully busy because that shows that my popularity is good and I am successful. That is the ultimate ambition of any actor. But once it becomes a compulsion, the mind revolts. You are no more interested in doing something which you are forced to do. I have started hating the entire system of acting, shooting etc.

There is so much pain hidden behind every person on the screen and behind the screen while making a movie . . .'

Aniket tapped on her shoulder in a consoling manner and said, 'don't worry . . . everything will be alright. Things will set right themselves at the right time.'

That night Aniket was wondering that how people compromised their priorities and relations in life for the sake of money. He also realized that he may not really understand it because he never felt shortage of money in his life.

*　　*　　*

Srikant was sweating profusely out of nervousness. He was just pacing up and down in the bedroom. His wife asked him, 'What is the problem Srikant? Are you not feeling well?' He just looked at her. How was he going to tell her the truth? His family members were not fully aware of his actual conduct. He had maintained a better-than-average image as a politician. There were few politicians in every parliament, who had a clean image. He could be counted as one among them.

His wife again asked him, 'anything serious? You are not normal . . .' Srikant just waved his hand in disapproving style saying, 'No . . . nothing. I just overate the dinner. You sleep . . . !' Srikant went to the terrace. He was evaluating various options in front of him. The first option was to make arrangement for the sum demanded by Deen Dayal and close the chapter. But there was no guarantee that the issue would be closed forever. It was like an allopathic medicine which treated the symptoms on short term basis with every chance of a recurrence in near future.

The other option was to dare Deen Dayal to make the revelations to the world. Srikant shuddered at the idea. He imagined the TV news giving out a breaking news about Srikant being caught in a sting operation accepting bribe for doing a favor. How his family would react to him? Would his children still respect him, after the revelations? Would he ever go to meet his old parents and face them looking in their eyes? Would he have the moral courage and strength to make speeches in large public gatherings, professing the eradication of corruption? How would he face the journalists who would probe the matter well beyond the investigating agencies?

Srikant regretted for allowing himself to be in such a situation. He pitied himself, saying that for past few months, he was voluntarily going to quit 'such' activities. Yet he was caught in this scam. Who would believe him if he said that he was already on the verge of becoming a clean politician? Destiny plays a cruel game sometimes. All his life he indulged in corrupt activities but was never caught. And now when he was mentally reformed and was about to mend his ways, he faced the biggest challenge of his life. His entire political future was at risk. His reputation, carefully built over several years was at stake.

He felt tired thinking of these thoughts. He had only two options and both were not very attractive. He did not realize when he slept on the sofa of his living room thinking about the future. He woke up in the morning and wondered how he could sleep under such stressful conditions. He thought that probably when a person's mind is extremely tired of thinking, he sleeps out of lack of energy to think anymore. He had a hurried breakfast and went to his office. He had to decide on something by evening. Letting the things to go as they were was not an option.

While sitting in his office, he made some quick calculations about the source of funds. He had accumulated enough assets in various forms to raise this amount at a short notice. The problem was that it was not a permanent solution. He needed a lasting solution to this mess. And his mind suddenly thought of an evil idea. How would it be, if he eliminated Deen Dayal? Though he did not know any contract killers nor he ever indulged in such activities, with some enquiries around, he would be able to arrange that. But the time was running out for him. He was nowhere near a good solution to his problem.

Srikant looked at the photos of Gods on the walls of his office. He needed some divine intervention now, as his mind was getting wild in absence of any way forward. He wondered whether Gods really existed and whether they had any powers to help the human beings at such crucial times. Unfortunately, he was not an A class devotee, by which he could expect Gods to descend and rescue him from the imbroglio. He knew his limitations as a devotee and was fully aware about God's limitations as well, to help him in an unreasonable case.

It was while he was having lunch in the office that he got a call from his wife. She said, his parents had come to his house. He was surprised. Did they know about this? Why did they come now? He respected his parents very much and always went home immediately on their arrival to be with them and talk to them. He had to follow the norm now too. He left the office in deep thoughts. On one side, his options were limited, his time was running out and now he was going to be busy in discharging his family obligations, which further pushed him away from a solution. He wondered what was happening to him in last few hours and why was it happening. He always believed that whatever happens, it happens for good. But here it was difficult to imagine what good would come out of this.

He reached his house and with great difficulty managed to keep normal expressions and behavior in front of his parents. They had met after few months and talked at length about all routine things around. His parents had no idea about the turmoil going through their son's mind. At one point, Srikant almost decided that harming Deen Dayal was the only good option and even picked up his phone to call his secretary to enquire about the modus operandi. But somehow he kept the phone down because the sane part of his mind did not allow him to do so.

Slowly the hands of clock were moving forward. Today, the hands appeared to be racing towards their goal post of 6 pm. Srikant was under intense pressure to act. Now his options were getting limited with each passing minute. There was no fresh call from Deen Dayal but the threat was same as before. He meant business when he spoke.

It was 6 pm and Srikant had not made any effort to either arrange any payment or plead Deen Dayal to give him some more time. He had spent all his time thinking of the consequences and did not make any move. He did not act because none of the options appealed to him. He was not so much worried about giving money, as he cared for his reputation. Now the only option left for him was to wait for 9 pm and see whether Deen Dayal executed his threat. It was a dreadful thought for Srikant because his father was in the habit of watching the 9 pm news every day without fail.

The family completed their dinner and was sitting in front of the 72 inch TV waiting for the news at 9 pm. The 30 seconds advertisements before start of the news appeared to be 30 minutes for Srikant who had almost given up on his future. In the next few minutes he would be discredited for accepting bribe and in all probabilities suspended from the party after he resigned from the post on 'moral' grounds. He was worried about his father's reaction on seeing the sting operation.

The news reader appeared on the screen and started off with breaking news. Srikant almost fainted in his seat.

The news reader read out the breaking news with a stoic face . . . 'Deen Dayal, a veteran politician is fighting for his life in a hospital following a serious road accident just outside a TV channel office on the outskirts of Delhi. A truck rammed the car in which he was travelling. Three other persons travelling with him were declared dead . . . .'

CHAPTER 13

One day Vikram woke up and found Vineetha still lying on the bed. Usually she used to wake up before him and prepare his favorite coffee, even in her adverse health conditions. He looked surprisingly at her and found that she was not looking normal. It appeared as if she was experiencing some kind of pain. He looked enquiringly at her, more with concern than anything else. She just indicated to him by her expressions that she was not feeling well. He immediately rushed her to the hospital.

The doctors checked her condition and admitted her in the ICU. Vikram was nervously waiting outside. The doctor came out soon and said that her condition was deteriorating fast and they needed to perform a surgery immediately. Any delay would be risky for her life. At the same time, the chances of success in the operation were not guaranteed either. They were bleak at best.

Vikram requested doctors to allow him to speak to his wife before the operation began. They agreed. Vikram rushed inside the operation theatre and stood by Vineetha's bed. She was looking pale in the white bed sheets of hospital. The sparkle from her face was missing. She sensed his arrival and half opened her eyes. He held her hand and looked assuringly at her. She had a faint smile on her face. He did not exactly understand the meaning of her smile.

Vineetha said in a fragile voice, 'Vikram, it is time now. Thanks for being the way you were all through . . . !'

Vikram felt his emotions rise suddenly. Tears came in his eyes. He did not say anything. His throat was too choked to utter even a single word.

Vineetha said, 'Vikram, it was a short time in this life. God willing I shall see you again in my next life. Please forgive me for all my silly and major mistakes which might have offended you.'

Vikram said, 'Vineetha, you will be alright. I do believe in miracles. You will get better and better . . .'

Vineetha said, 'Vikram there is not enough time to talk now. Take good care of yourselves. And remember; please remarry if you feel the need for a companion. I won't feel bad. Everyone has a right to live the life the way one wants . . .'

Vikram was about to say something when his attention was distracted by the team of doctors who were by now prepared to start the operation. They both looked at each other the last time and he came out of the operation theatre.

Suddenly Vikram felt as though he wanted to tell her so many things, which he missed telling her. And he realized, he may never get an opportunity now to say it to her. He regretted it. He could not reverse time and let her know his feelings and thoughts. After four hours of operation, doctors came out grim faced and patted on Vikram's shoulder with those fearful words, 'We are sorry. We could not save her.'

Vikram was emotionless for a few minutes. While he had been expecting this for some time now, when the moment arrived, he was left clueless. He suddenly felt a big void in his life as if it was cut into two pieces. The second piece was snatched away from him. His near and dear ones who had come to the hospital started consoling him and remembering Vineetha and all her good qualities. On hearing this sad news, his old friends Srikant and Amit also came to his house immediately to offer their condolences. Pankaj called him from America to share his grief. They tried to console him, but could not take away his pain. He kept on weeping uncontrollably. These moments are very difficult in life, and one cannot escape from them. Vikram was feeling every moment that Vineetha would come out from kitchen or from the balcony. He felt that she would have been extremely happy to meet his childhood friends. She had met all of them in their marriage earlier.

Vikram was not sure how he was going to spend even a moment in his house without Vineetha. She had been an integral part of his life. Her presence used to make the atmosphere lively and vibrant in the house. Without her, it would be too dull and boring to live in that house. Vikram started spending time outside the house, going to movies, libraries, parks, malls and sometimes he just strolled on the roads to pass time. His condition became almost hysterical. The intensity of his thoughts did not diminish with time. He started growing beard. He started reading all philosophical literature in libraries. He started discovering subtle interlinks between the philosophy, mythology and management.

He read that Abraham Lincoln too was madly in love with a girl before his marriage. However, the girl died untimely and Abraham Lincoln went into a big depression for several months. He went almost crazy remembering her all the time and spending most of his time on her grave. He wrote some of the most philosophical poems during that period, which are considered classics even today. The punch line of one of the poem read, 'Oh Mortal . . . how can you be proud of anything in this world . . .' Vikram was too moved by this line. He agreed with it. What was the value of any sort of arrogance or pride when no one was certain about one's life or time of death?

Mankind may have landed on moon and may reach Mars in the near future, but it will never be able to conquer death. That is the inevitable truth.

*   *   *

Rahul was very happy to take his parents for sightseeing in and around Manhattan. Every place they visited was unique in one way or the other and reflected a part of some history. The obvious difference again was the cleanliness at such spots and the kind of visitors. In a stark contrast, most of the Indian monuments had some irrelevant scribbling on the wall and were not neatly maintained.

Soon after settling down in the new place, Pankaj had started going for morning and evening walks in a nearby park. His logic was that his body needed some exercise on a daily basis to remain fit and healthy. At this age, walking was the only exercise which he could do without having the risk of getting hurt or strained. He was fully aware that in another few years, he may need a walking stick and he wanted to postpone that day as farther as possible.

During his routine morning walks, Pankaj used to sit for a while after 5 rounds of the 'walking track', on a particular bench in the park, facing the main road. And he used to see the traffic on the road. The posh cars used to travel in a disciplined manner on smooth roads without honking at all. He wondered how they travelled without honking, as in India occasional honking is a must while driving the cars. He also observed that people followed the traffic rules happily. People stopped at the red signal and they did not change the lanes abruptly. And to his further surprise, he also noticed that many of the drivers were Indians. If they were abiding by the law so well in US, what stopped them in following the same discipline in India? He had no answer.

He also wondered how the individual reference mattered in a given situation. While he was sitting there in the park, the people on the road were rushing to their offices. At the same time, children were going to the school. Office goers were hurrying to arrive at the office on time, while the businessmen were out with new determination to get new business. The brilliant children looked forward for an enjoyable day at school while the back benchers were worried about the remaining homework or the pending assignments.

The world remained same, while the individual reference made it look different to each one of them. The world from the eyes of a successful businessman would be much different from the world seen by a beggar. The definition of life, happiness, world etc would therefore differ from person to person, based on his birth, upbringing and achievements in life.

One day while he sat on a bench after his usual round of walks, he observed another Indian old man sitting beside him. He introduced himself to the old man and they began talking. The old man was one Mr. Chari who was staying with his son. After the initial talk about 'where are you from, in India' and 'where do you stay here' the discussion wandered on the culture of US. Pankaj was new to US anyway, so he was only listening while Chari did most of the talking. From his talk, Pankaj understood that the culture of US was way different from Indian culture. In India, the parents took care of their children till they were settled in their lives. The parent's responsibility included complete education of the sons and daughters plus a job for the son and marriage of daughter were the minimum milestones to be achieved while they travelled together in life. After that, either they continued to stay together or stayed separately depending on the circumstances and individual personalities.

In a stark contrast, in US, the parents encouraged their children to be 'independent' at a tender age of 18. That meant the children stayed separately. And the circle was completed when children would not look after their ageing parents in their old age and admitted them into various old age homes. Pankaj felt pity for the young children as well as the old parents in US. He felt that they missed living a life based on personal relations, understanding and cooperation. Instead their lives were more or less commercial devoid of any sentiments, feelings or emotions attached.

Thereafter, every time Pankaj spotted an old man in a mall or a shop or on streets, he would sympathetically look at him and think, how much suffering he must be going through. He did not like the culture. He felt that old people were the pride and moral support for any house because they had seen more rainy seasons and were wise with experience. It was nothing short of a crime to leave them in old age homes.

Another big difference which Pankaj observed in US was that the life was too mechanical out there. Strangers did not wish on the streets while acquaintances did not bother to speak a few words when came across. He remembered back home, every person would stop and enquire a few things with affection before moving on, when came across on the streets. Pankaj wondered what the meaning in life was when people behaved like machines without any emotions and attachments. He suddenly felt as though he was living in a society of domesticated animals. He felt so, because animals do not have the capacity to express their emotions clearly. Most of the Indians had come to US by leaving their near and dear ones behind in India, yet they were not ready to mix with one another in US. This was like feeling thirsty, yet preferring to live in the ocean and say that there is no sweet water around to drink.

He wondered how the country was considered as a developed one and a superpower at that! Did the human values not count on the path of progress? And if it was so, what was the use of such a progress? In his opinion, an underdeveloped country with people possessing human values was far superior to a developed country with mechanical emotionless people. What was a country after all? A country was nothing but a land with boundaries. The country gets its social standing based on the people who inhabit that land. The generations pass on their values and beliefs to the younger ones.

However, once in a while a person is born in every country that changes the fate of millions of people of that period and subsequent generations. These people wield extraordinary influence over masses with their strong ideologies. Some of them are Martin Luther King, Mahatma Gandhi and Nelson Mandela. Then there are some who with their negative qualities have inflicted several emotional scars on the population of that country. Some of them are Hitler, Mussolini and Saddam Hussain. Countless people have lost their lives or spent it in prison for no fault of theirs. Today, these countries carry the burden of their negative legacy, even decades after they have gone.

One day, while Pankaj was in a supermarket, suddenly a young Indian man came from nowhere and touched his feet. He was surprised. People around too were looking with amusement. When the boy got up, Pankaj recognized him. Yes, he was Alok, one of the bright students of Pankaj's school several years ago. Alok respectfully asked, 'Guruji, remember me? I am Alok, one of your students in 1998. Pankaj exclaimed, 'Alok, how can we teachers forget about our good students? How come you are here?' Alok replied like an excited child, 'Guruji, after I left your school, I went to Mumbai for higher education and then came here for my masters. Now I am working here as Computer engineer.' Pankaj was very happy at the success of his pupil and also felt grateful that he still had retained his humility to not only accost him but also to respectfully touch his feet at a public place. A really learned person always retains his humility irrespective of the changing circumstances. Pankaj was very happy that evening.

Slowly Pankaj started feeling homesick. This was not his age to feel homesick, yet he remembered his village and the people. He desperately wished to breathe the fresh air of his village fields. He felt thirsty of drinking the pure water from the wells in Shantinagar. He longed to feel the warmth of the people in his Shantinagar. The craze about living for a few days in a foreign land had vanished.

India was calling him.

*   *   *

Amit was sad that Aniket had to taste failure so early in his life. He believed that a person should experience failure, as it makes the person strong. He personally believed that any failure which did not break him, made him stronger. However, he did not want his son to experience it, because he loved him very much. He had brought up Aniket by providing him every possible comfort and happiness which he asked for. Therefore, he was not very happy at the turn of events, when after a first unexpected success Aniket had to face two failures in Bollywood.

He even wondered whether he should ask Aniket to quit Bollywood and join him in his business. But he was not sure how Aniket would react to this proposal. There was a possibility that he could view it as an insult, or he could take it as a negative feedback for his performance so far. At the worst, he may even get demotivated and go into a depression. Amit did not want that to happen. At least he did not want to be a reason for any such thing happening to Aniket. After some thought, he decided to leave Aniket as it is for a few more days, as time was the biggest heal for any human tragedy. God has blessed mankind with this great quality that the intensity of a person's happiness or sadness diminishes with time. If the intensity remained same forever, then people would not be able to live, out of extreme happiness or sadness. When one loses a loved one, he feels terribly dejected. However, the intensity of his emotions reduces after a week. It is much lower after a month or a year. Similarly, the emotions of happiness also reduce and people start leading their daily lives as if nothing has happened. Perhaps, this quality enables people to experience new happiness and sadness as the life progresses from birth to death uninterrupted.

One day while Amit was going to office in his posh car driven by his uniformed chauffeur, a small boy came begging to his car at a traffic signal. Usually, while travelling in the car in Mumbai, he worked on his laptop about the various presentations, proposals and financial statements so as to utilize his time efficiently. And by doing this, he believed that he could tap more time out of his busy schedules enabling him to make more informed and better decisions. However, that day, for some reason, he just sat quietly looking out of the window. The begging child was in torn and unkempt clothes with overgrown hair covering large portion of his forehead. Yet there was innocence in the child's eyes as he looked pleadingly at Amit. Somehow Amit, who ignored this normally, had a change of mind and gave the boy a Ten Rupees note by slightly lowering the window and closing it back again. The boy looked at Amit with a deep feeling of thankfulness. His happiness was reflected on his beaming face and gleaming eyes. The boy folded his hands in a 'Namaskar' and thanked Amit. The traffic signal turned Green and the car moved on.

Amit wondered how cheap the boy's happiness was. In fact he wondered how the definition of happiness varied from person to person. A beggar on the street would be thrilled to get food twice a day. His circumstances did not allow him to think or worry about anything beyond the next few hours. The words planning, budget and savings had no relevance to his lifestyle. He wondered at God's scheme of things. All are living in one world. All are having a limited appetite. All move on the same roads. Yet, some people strive for food while some others strive for something else.

Amit reached office and started reviewing files about a meeting next day, when his driver came with his brief case and laptop bag. After keeping it there, he stood there as if hesitating to say something. Amit realized it and asked him, 'What happened, Sitaram? You want something?'

Sitaram cleared his throat and said looking downward, 'Saheb, my son has completed his graduation. I wanted to get him some job. But he does not want to work. He wants to start a business instead.'

Amit suddenly felt the irony. He desperately wanted his son to carry on his established business as its heir but he had no interest in running a business and here was his driver's son willing to start his own business.

Amit looked with mixed feelings at Sitaram and asked, 'So, What help do you expect from me Sitaram?'

Sitaram again looked down and said, 'Saheb, he needs some money to start the business. He needs Rs. 2 Lakhs.' Sitaram was not sure whether his demand would be met.

Amit reflected for a while and said, 'Sitaram, you have been working with me for the past several years. You have driven my car for all my business meetings and schedules. On many occasions, while returning late in the evenings from outstation assignments, I used to sleep off in the car leaving the safety of my life in your hands. You have worked under all conditions with devotion. I think it is time for me to repay some of it today. I have paid you a monthly salary for the work done by you. But I need to repay you for the extra dedication and sincerity displayed by you in your work, which has to come from within a person and cannot be quantified in a job description or any contract. Please ask accountant Murthy to come in. I shall advise him to arrange Rupees Two Lakhs for your son. My best wishes for your son's business.'

Sitaram had tears in his eyes. He folded his hands and thanked Amit for his kind gesture. He left the room. Amit felt happy for some reasons. He did not know whether it was because he helped someone start his own business or it was because he was able to repay Sitaram's years of service, or he was seeing a young Amit in Sitaram's son. Once again it struck in his mind that the definition of happiness varied from person to person. Sitaram's son would be the happiest man today because he got the much needed financial support to start his business.

In the afternoon the same day, a delegation came to his office from a charitable trust asking him for donation. He told them that he did not mind giving them some money, but wanted to know what they did with the money received from all such contributions/donations. The leader of the delegation, a gentle person wearing spectacles with a round frame and white hair said, 'Sir, we use this money to help the underprivileged people of the society. Our volunteers regularly visit the railway stations and temples where they search for young orphan children begging and in poor conditions. These children are brought to our ashram and given shelter and good education so that they can succeed in life. After all, they too have an equal right to live in this society with honor and pride instead of living the life of hatred, ostracism and criticism. We also have a separate section in our ashram where we house the old people abandoned by their grown up children. The old people need to spend the last days of their lives in a good environment rather than suffering the feeling of being abandoned and uncared for. We provide proper medical facilities for them and arrange religious discourses every evening as they would be mostly interested in those topics during this part of their life.'

Amit was lost in a different world. Suddenly he felt a deep satisfaction just by listening to the person. He felt happy to see that there existed someone in the society who did these extremely noble works without any rewards whatsoever, except the blessings of people positively affected by the people helped by them. He had an urge to be associated with this kind of an activity. He had made lot of money. He had started his business empire and grown it to a respectable size. His desire for earning more and more money was satisfied long time ago. Now he had reached a stage where money was no more an enticing factor in his life. He had suddenly found a new direction in his otherwise stagnant life.

He wanted to become a philanthropist. He wanted to help as many people as he could. He wanted to bring a smile on as many people's face as possible. He realized that he owed this gesture to the society which had given him so much by way of money, respect and honor. He wondered why he did not get this idea before. He considered his life was wasted for past few years when he could have started involving in these activities much before. He lost an opportunity to help many people during these years. He did not want to delay anymore now.

While he was going home, an old Raj Kapoor song was playing on radio . . . 'Kisiki muskurahaton pe ho nisar . . . kisika dard ho sake to le udhar . . . kisike vaaste ho tere dil me pyar . . . . Jeena isika naam hai . . . !'

*   *   *

Srikant was shocked to see on television the tragic news about Deen Dayal's accident. He had not instructed anyone to go and harm Deen Dayal. Then how did this happen? Was it an intervention of God to rescue him from his problem? He was not sure whether God harmed someone to save someone else from a problem. Nevertheless, he felt relieved at this unexpected turn of events. He wiped the sweat off his face and drank two glasses of water. He had a lifeline now. His immediate problem was postponed by the forces of nature. He had time to think and take a decision.

The next day, more details of the accident were revealed. A truck had lost control and came in the opposite direction resulting in a head on collision with Deen Dayal's car. Deen Dayal's legs had suffered multiple fractures and in all probabilities, the legs needed to be amputated to save him. Deen Dayal would never be able to walk again on his legs. Doctors were trying to see whether artificial legs could be fitted so that he could at least stand and walk slowly. But the chances appeared remote as both legs were equally affected.

The following week, Srikant went to the hospital with a bouquet of flowers with the tag 'Get well soon'. By then, Deen Dayal was stable and recovering. People were allowed to meet him. The media persons clicked photographs as Srikant walked into the hospital. Srikant kept a sad face in front of the media and said that he had come to see Deen Dayal and wish him a speedy recovery.

Srikant managed to get some moments of privacy with Deen Dayal. He was eager to listen to him and know whether he carried on with the threat or forgot about it. Moreover, he wanted to make it clear to Deen Dayal that he had not planted this accident. He wanted to sincerely sympathize with him as well. After all, they were from the same 'biradari' and any such thing happening to anyone of them was sad.

Deen Dayal looked calm. He slowly opened his eyes and looked at Srikant. Srikant kept the bouquet near the table and sat on a chair kept beside the bed. He held Deen Dayal's hand and said, 'Deen Dayal ji, how are you feeling now?'

Deen Dayal just nodded that he was feeling better.

Srikant added after a pause, 'Deen Dayal ji, I just wanted to inform you that I did not carry out that accident. You may mistake me . . .'

Deen Dayal interrupted in a slow feeble voice, 'Srikant ji, I know you very well. You would not do this to me. You are not that bad . . .'

Srikant suddenly felt a rush of emotions within him. Here was his detractor, who had tried black mailing him just a few days back, was now expressing his confidence in the positive side of him.

There was an awkward pause, as neither had any right words for the moment.

Srikant said, 'Deen Dayal ji, thanks for that . . . I shall give you the money soon. Sorry, I could not make arrangements within the deadline set by you.'

Deen Dayal had a faint smile on his face. He said, 'Srikant ji, forget about it. What will I do with money now?'

Srikant did not quite understand.

Deen Dayal continued, 'Srikant ji, now my value is reduced to zero in politics. Our political system values and respects only those who can win elections for the party and have capability to save the party from crisis. The moment one loses this capability, he is automatically thrown out of the system. I have learnt that already there is a fight within our party to replace me as the leader of opposition. Also, the potential candidates are getting ready to contest the elections next year from my constituency. Very few have bothered to come and meet me. Even I heard my two sons are fighting to take over my seat while I have still not officially vacated it. It pains me to see that they are spending more time fighting about my legacy than looking after me when I am still around, that too in a bad condition.'

Srikant felt very sad at this state of Deen Dayal. He said, 'Deen Dayal ji, no no . . . you will become alright. I am sure you will continue to flourish in your party for years to come . . .'

Deen Dayal said, 'Srikant ji, so kind of you. But it is only a wishful thinking. I am taking a Sanyas not only from my political life but also from my personal life. Now I shall only live till my death. I have no more ambitions left. God has punished me for which sin I committed I don't know. I only hope that I get a good death. I don't wish to live longer in this condition, where people have to look after me and my life becomes dependent on others for even my daily chores in life.'

Srikant was speechless. Here was a firebrand leader of opposition, lying on bed and wishing for an early death. One accident had changed his entire thought process. His attitude, his vision of life had completely changed. Srikant could not make out whether Deen Dayal was being a pessimist or just a realist. It was difficult to say.

One thing was sure . . . Srikant had to implement his plan of being honest with immediate effect. There was no time left for him. He was not sure whether something like Deen Dayal was going to happen to him, but he wanted to be ready in case it happens. He did not want to regret later.

Srikant returned from the hospital feeling a bit guilty . . . because, an accident had almost reformed Deen Dayal while he still needed to expiate for his sins.

CHAPTER 14

—⚬⚬⚬—

Vikram read lots of books on Philosophy and almost redefined the meaning of words like happiness, life, achievement etc. According to his revised definitions, a person would experience true happiness only when he makes others happy. By helping someone who is in need . . . The real meaning of life was to spread happiness around and help in making a better environment for others to live in. The life of a person is considered meaningful when he lives for others and not just for oneself.

Vikram took a long time to recover from the loss of Vineetha. In her memory, he started a Cancer hospital and provided free treatment to the poor patients. Anybody could walk into the hospital and get treatment, however costly it might be. He had chosen the best doctors for treatment and procured the most advanced equipments.

He wondered that mankind had not been able to so far reason out why cancer happened and also its definite cure. He felt sad that the entire world's best medical brains cannot save a cancer patient. What criteria did God use while selecting people to suffer from cancer? Was it their previous birth's sins? Or this was just unluck-by-chance? Why does everyone not get an equal opportunity to enjoy this world for full time? Why do some people have to leave early when the show is still on? His mind used to go numb with these thoughts, which occurred in his mind at least half a dozen times every day since Vineetha's death.

Vikram lost the fire of motivating others in his lectures and speeches. Earlier, his presentation would focus on the amazing powers of mind and limitless opportunities of a person which would instantly inspire a person to achieve greater results through a better performance. However, now these words, phrases and anecdotes were being replaced by philosophical thoughts like, 'What did we bring here, that we shall take away with us?', 'Amassing personal wealth is not a noble thing' or 'However high one may rise in life, one finally rests in a graveyard somewhere on earth' etc. As a result, he started getting less invitations for his talks. Instead his name started getting popular in the religious circles. His audience group changed from ambitious executives to the elderly and pious people who valued the philosophical ideas more in life.

He started visiting a nearby temple in the evenings where a group of people used to wait for him to know more about philosophy and values of life. The people treated him like some baba or a learned person. They narrated their personal problems to him and intently listened to the solutions offered by him. Most of the time, his solutions appeared to be highly logical, correct and productive to them.

One day, an old man asked him, 'Swamiji, when the twin towers were attacked in US, some 3700 people were dead. Were all of them sinners? Definitely not! Then why did they get such a horrific death by burning and then get buried inside the huge debris without as much even having the fate of the last rites performed in prescribed ways by their near and dear ones? Does God not differentiate between a sinner and a saint?'

Vikram sighed and went into a deep thought. The question was very valuable indeed. There had to be some difference between a sinner and a saint. Otherwise, people would stop valuing the noble qualities of living and would take to the easy road filled with vices. He had no ready answer for this question. However, he tried to explain it as much as possible.

Vikram said, 'We are too shortsighted to know and judge whether the death was good or bad for those people. There were hundreds of people who had accidentally entered that building for business reasons only on that fateful day, while there were many other people working as regular staff in offices in those towers who were absent that day. Some of them were even late by few minutes and escaped the mishap. For those people who were not leading a happy life, it was a sort of 'mukti' to have died in one instant. Also, we do not know the life after death. May be it is much more beautiful that this life on earth. So, for the good people, it might be God's strategy to lift them up faster as a reward for them to start that 'afterlife' earlier. That way, they can avoid the miseries associated with this life on earth. As Bhagwad Gita says, 'Every human being has to go through the four events—Janma, Mrityu, Jara and Vyadhi which means Birth, Death, Old age and Diseases. No one is exempt from them. So such incidents give God an opportunity to shift the blessed ones on a fast track to the future unknown to mankind.'

Everyone was keenly listening to this brilliant question and the equally mystifying answer. Someone else asked, 'Swamiji, 'What is destiny? Is everything including death destined? There is another theory which says that we are the creators of our own destiny. So, which is correct?'

Vikram once again dwelled over the question for a few seconds and then said, 'Both the theories are partially correct. God has neither kept everything to himself nor has he given complete freedom to the people. He has not kept the full control with himself because, if that were so, people would not do any karma. For example, a student will not study because, if he is destined to pass he will pass anyway. And if he is destined to fail he will fail anyway, however much he may study. So, it works as a disincentive in both ways, for those who want to work, as well as those who are lazy.'

The concept was slowly sinking in everyone's mind.

Vikram continued, 'Similarly, God has not given full control of the destiny to mankind. Because then, a time would come when they will challenge death, they will challenge God's existence, they will stop respecting the mighty nature itself. And also, in such a scenario, the powerful ones would assume the role of God as with their efforts they can do almost anything.'

People were puzzled. If it was neither this nor that, then what was the truth?

Vikram said in an enlightening tone, 'God plays a game of rummy with all of us. He deals the quota of 13 cards to each one of us at the start of the game. Thereafter, he plays according to how we play. The cards thrown by him are based on which cards we throw. That means if we make sincere efforts, if we are good to others, if we help others . . . in short, if we follow the path advised by him then he will also do good for us. However, if we are not, then he will not provide enough opportunities for us. We can't expect him to help us without initially making any efforts from our side. If we keep only praying God and visiting the places of worship, he would not help us. He wants us to first show enthusiasm and also to make sincere effort to achieve what we desire. Then he comes to our rescue. Similarly, he would not go and help those who try to do things on their own, without looking at him for help.

There was another young person listening carefully all along, who seemed to have some doubts and was looking for an opportunity to ask and get an answer.

He asked, 'Swamiji, why do we see that some righteous people suffer throughout their lives while some bad people have all the luxuries in their life. How is that possible? Why is God not fair in distributing happiness?'

Again Vikram went into deep thoughts. He said, 'When you sow a seed of mango, you get a mango tree after certain period. Similarly, when you sow an apple tree, you get an apple tree after a certain period. Similarly, every Karma done by us has a reward associated with it. Good Karma generates good rewards while bad Karma results in bad results. One cannot sow a seed of Mango and expect Apples from the tree. Now, the time after which the rewards come to us also differ and vary with different types of Karma, just as different seeds take different periods of time to develop into a fruit bearing tree. When a person does a karma which is scheduled to give him the rewards after say 5 years, but dies after only two years, then the rewards of that karma get accrued to the next janma. The same soul keeps changing bodies just as we keep changing clothes. That explains why you find this discrepancy about the deeds not matching with the rewards in some cases.'

A middle aged person asked, 'Swamiji, what is the secret of happiness?'

Vikram smiled and replied, 'To answer this question, you need to first define happiness. What is happiness? Incidentally, the definition of happiness varies from person to person. In spite of that you will never see any person completely happy in this world. As Swami Ramdas says, 'Jagi sarva sukhi asa kon ahe?' It is a beautiful verse in Marathi which means 'Is there anyone who is completely happy in this world?' The verse further says, 'Ask your own mind and you will realize that you will not find a single person who is completely happy in this world'. Everyone has his share of problems.

However, to answer your question briefly, yes there is a secret of happiness. Among all the qualities which go in making a person happy, the two topmost qualities are 'needs' and 'expectations'. One should have minimum needs to be happy. If you have a cycle, you will need a scooter, if you have a scooter, you will need a car and so on. If you have one house, you will need a bigger house. The human needs are endless. Even a king wants to keep adding to his territories. Knowing well that no one is going to take away anything from this world, people still keep accumulating and expecting to add to their possessions. So, if a person is able to restrict and reduce his needs, he will be happy.'

Vikram continued, 'And the second quality is regarding expectations. One should have minimum expectations from others. It is the high expectations which give rise to all the disappointments in this world. Do not expect that the other person is going to treat you in a first class way. Then you will be happy. At least there will be no disappointment. Please note that when people do not behave as per your expectations, it is not that they do not like you. It could be just that they are simply not aware of your expectations. While at some other times, they may have different priorities. Each individual has his own priorities and preferences. No one should expect that others behave and act the way you want them to. Such feelings will only add bitterness to the relations.'

'Even if you are able to reduce your needs and are able to lower your expectations from others, you have crossed halfway mark on the road to happiness.'

*   *   *

Pankaj spent the remaining days in US just for the sake of his grandson. He observed that the hospitals observed far more hygiene than in India. He wondered how the children in India grew up in not so clean environments yet were quite normal. As the days of his return to India neared, he felt an excitement, which did not suit his age. He was thrilled like a child to be back home soon. True, old age is but a shadow of the childhood. In both these phases, one is more dependent on others. Also, one has to learn to compromise and adjust with others during these phases, as not everything will happen according to one's desires. The only difference would be that in childhood, one looks toward the future with lot of aspirations and dreams in eyes, while in old age, one looks at the past with memories of all the beautiful moments in his heart.

The plane landed in Mumbai and Pankaj had tears in his eyes involuntarily as the emotions ran high inside him at the thought of coming back to Matrubhoomi. Actually, he faced no difficulties in US to feel so great about returning back, yet for some reasons he was becoming emotional. Probably he believed that our imperfection is better than other's perfection. His luggage came out just in time and they were surprised to get a warm reception from Vasudev Rao and two others from his village. They hugged each other like he was returning after winning a world cup. There was a genuine happiness on their faces. Pankaj was happy to express his emotions so freely in a public place by hugging all of them, which was a bit uncommon in US.

They returned to Shantinagar and almost everyone from the village came to their house to enquire about their well being and to hear from them their experiences of US. Pankaj had narrated all his experiences in detail to everyone almost repeating many things over and over again. Neither was he tired of repeating it nor was his wife tired of preparing snacks, tea for all the visitors.

Once again, his routine started and the news of his foreign trip became old enough for people not to refer to it actively during the general discussions.

He was living a life of satisfaction. He had lived the life exactly as he wanted. At the peak of his tuitions business, he had taken a bold decision to leave it all and try to help the underprivileged children of a village. His move was going to reduce his financial income drastically. Yet he plunged into it. He knew that no amount of money would make a person happy, if he was not truly happy doing the things he did for his livelihood. On the contrary, a little money or even no money would immensely satisfy him, if he had passion for the things he did. And he heard to the inner voice. He left the comforts of a city life and spent the prime period of his active life to develop the children of Shantinagar. He would shudder at the thought that without his efforts, the thousands of children whom he taught and provided quality education over the years, would have ended up as either laborers in the village fields or at best workers in some nearby industries. Each one of his student had carved a better life for himself through the values instilled by Pankaj in him. They were responsible citizens of India who differentiated between good and bad. They desisted from doing bad things. They were the righteous people in society, who improved the goodness factor of societies in which they settled around the world. This was Pankaj's biggest contribution to his country and fellow countrymen. He was a deeply satisfied person today.

Few people get to live the life in the way they wanted. Pankaj was one of them. The path chosen by him was not glamorous nor was it financially rewarding. Yet it was immensely satisfying him.

*   *   *

Ever since the thought of philanthropy came to Amit's mind, his thought process changed. He was now not so aggressive in his business expansion or future projections. He slowly delegated his responsibilities to his senior team members and started learning about the philanthropists in the world. He realized that many successful businessmen turned philanthropists in their old age. He remembered having read somewhere that Azim Premji had donated around Rupees Eight Thousand Crores for setting up and developing primary schools in rural areas all over India. He wondered whether it was some kind of their despair which led them to philanthropy or it was a stark feeling that they cannot continue to work with same stamina in their advanced ages. In his case, was it Aniket's refusal to lead his business which has strengthened his philanthropic aspirations?

He realized one thing. Beyond a certain stage in life, money ceases to be a motivating factor. When one has earned enough money for his basic needs and some luxuries, the balance money is either reinvested or kept in banks or worst hidden as black money. Unfortunately, majority of the population in this world never come to this stage in their life time. They need to continuously keep working to earn their daily bread. If their monthly salary stops for three months, they are in trouble in fourth month. Therefore, they never come to this stage of experiencing the 'financial freedom'. Many creative ideas get buried in the pursuit of making two ends meet. The only thing abundantly available in this world is wasted talent. There are several people in this world who are capable of doing wonders, if only their financial needs are taken care of. Amit wanted to be a change agent in such people's lives.

One day, he called a board meeting and advised them that he shall be transferring the responsibility of running the day to day operations to the next in hierarchy and also apprised them of his plans to spend time and money on philanthropic activities. They all welcomed his move. In the next few months, Amit funded several hospitals in remote villages where no medical facilities were available. He started primary schools in several interior villages. He offered financial rewards for the poor meritorious students in various schools and colleges. He set up emergency relief centers to help the needy people in emergencies like earth quake, cyclones, floods or droughts. The fast changing nature was bringing such calamities at an alarming pace than ever before. He used to personally ensure that the help reached the needy people in time. That brought him a lot of satisfaction.

He had found a purpose in life. He wanted to spend rest of his life helping as many people as he could. He knew that when a person leaves this place, he does not carry with him a single rupee. All his estate, assets, money etc remain here. What only goes with him is the intangible powerful asset—that of blessings and good will. He wanted to earn it as much as possible. He valued the blessings of even a beggar at the traffic signal. He had devised a novel idea to ensure that his donations, contributions are spent in appropriate manner. Most of the time, he used to donate in kind rather than in cash. For example, he used to feed the poor people every day. He gave blankets to the people in huts who were shivering in cold nights. He gave books and notebooks to the children from poor families and rewarded them when they passed their exams.

*   *   *

Srikant was a changed man now. He had experienced too much anxiety in past few days. He did not want to subject himself to such temptations and guilt feelings again in future. However, he was trapped in a quagmire from where few have come out successfully unscathed. There were very few politicians existing who had no corruption charges against them. Most of the politicians left politics because they died, or they lost their authority in the party or they were caught in some scandals. The power of politics was so addictive that he found many politicians in their seventies and eighties still fighting elections and occupying ministries. He wondered what contribution they made in developing the society when their biggest concern would be to keep their health in a reasonably good condition.

He wanted to be a path breaker. He wanted to do something which was done by nobody before. He wanted to leave politics while he still commanded authority in the party and had age on his side. He wanted to lead a life of satisfaction without any guilt conscience. And the only way he could do it was to leave politics on a good note.

After long deliberation, he sent a note to his party high command that he wished to resign. The high command was surprised at this unexpected move from Srikant. Usually, no one left a seat of power unless compelled by circumstances. There was a flurry of activities in the party headquarters when everyone learnt about his move to quit. Some speculated that he was joining the rival party. Yet they could not substantiate the wiseness of such an absurd looking move.

Srikant was looking at his colleagues and everyone around in the party meetings with a new look in his eyes. He sort of pitied them that they were so blinded by power. He felt that he was someone different from others. Unfortunately, everyone around him thought that he had developed some mental problems and was becoming insane to throw away such a plum ministry and power. It is said that in a mental asylum, the doctors look at the patients with a pity in their eyes. At the same time, the patients look at doctors with a pity in their eyes thinking that they are actually good people and the doctor is in fact crazy. It all depended on from which angle one looked at the things around him. And sometimes, the mad people are considered happy because they are neither aware nor do they bother about the numerous problems created by 'wise' people affecting the whole world today.

CHAPTER 15

————— ∞∞∞ —————

It was a very special day in Pankaj's life. He had invited his old friends Amit, Srikant and Vikram for celebrating his 60ᵗʰ birthday in Shantinagar. And they had accepted his invitation. He was in high spirits from last one week with the thoughts of being a host to his childhood friends. After their school days, they had dispersed like scattered pearls from a necklace whose connecting thread was cut. Though they had met in between at times, it was only during some functions and for a short time. Now, all of them were relatively free and could afford to spend some time together without worrying about any deadline for assignments or meetings.

The happiness in Pankaj's mind was visible to the villagers who were witnessing a spring in his steps for last one week. When they asked him about it, he had replied,

'My friends are coming to visit me. We have grown up together. We have fought with one another, we shared some good times enjoying one another's success. Perhaps now is the time to evaluate who has achieved what in life.'

Srikant, Vikram and Amit came together in Amit's big SUV used by him on special occasions. They too looked excited to come to meet Pankaj in his village. They had started from Mumbai early in the morning and so reached Shantinagar by 10 am. Pankaj made them sit on white plastic chairs placed in his front yard and offered them hot tea. The tea tasted very special as it was made using the fresh unadulterated milk. Even the naturally cooled water served in steel glasses tasted sweet to them. The cool breeze made the atmosphere very pleasant.

Pankaj said, 'I am so grateful to you guys for accepting my invitation and coming here. For some time now, I was thinking that we should meet, as it has been a long time since we talked in a relaxed manner.'

Amit said, 'Pankaj, I envy you. The life seems so beautiful here. There is no pollution of whatsoever kind. The air is fresh, water is pure, and no traffic jams etc.'

Srikant said, 'Yes. He is enjoying his life here. While we are developing the nation by forming policies through constitutional process, he is making the grassroots strong with his efforts.'

Vikram said, 'True Srikant. There is a slight difference though . . . and that is in the genuineness of the cause. You do it for power. He does it for a purpose.'

Pankaj interrupted them and said, 'Guys, please do not start it all over again. We are in our sixties . . . grow up. Till when will you keep fighting?

Amit said, 'Agree with Pankaj. We have met after so many years. Let us know more about one another rather than arguing about our principles and perceptions.'

So it was decided that each one of them narrate their past experiences of life. They would reveal how life had treated them and what lessons they learnt from life. They all had a common beginning as schoolmates in Mumbai in seventies. Life had taken them on different routes after their graduation. While they had been meeting one another at times, this was a unique occasion when all of them met together and also that they were more relaxed now than they were ever before. They were in their sixties.

Srikant started off, 'Let me take you back to our teenage. Remember, I was left jobless saddled with a degree which did not fetch me any job? It was by chance that I happened to get closer to Sukhram and he spotted the 'talent' within me. He inducted me into the party as an ordinary worker. Initially I was given charge of mobilizing the youth from all colleges for rallies and bandhs. Soon I was getting recognized in the party circles and was fortunate enough to get the party ticket for the position of a corporater. And then the assembly and Parliament were not very far. I knew the power centers within the party and always kept them in good humor. There were times, when I collected large sums of money from people in the name of party fund and passed it on to these power centers for their personal usage.'

Srikant was sounding as though he was in a confession mode. Others were genuinely listening to him. After all, he was a big politician of their times.

Srikant continued, 'I enjoyed power. It made me feel absolutely wonderful to move in white bulletproof cars by stopping the traffic along all the arteries, while speeding in a cavalcade on empty roads. I had the power. The real power . . . ! I could do anything. I needed to go to the public only once in Five years during the elections. Thereafter, I had a free run till next elections.'

Pankaj asked him, 'Why did you retire so early from politics, Srikant?'

Srikant suddenly came to present from the past. He said, 'My life was changed when I was almost caught in a scandal. My opponent did a sting operation on me and was blackmailing me. I still remember those few hours I spent when I was in a tremendous dilemma as to what should I do? For the first time, I felt afraid of facing my father who happened to be with me during those days. I experienced fear of losing the respect, love and reputation in one go from everyone around me, including my parents, wife and children. It was a miracle which saved me and the sting operation did not see the light of the day. God had been exceptionally benevolent to me. However, it changed my attitude thereafter. I could sense the helplessness of Deen Dayal on a wheel chair. A very active politician was grounded by an accident. He became immobile. All his dreams and ambitions came to an abrupt end. What could he do with all the wealth he had, when he could not even walk a few steps? And it was painful to see how the near and dear ones turn away in times of crisis. His own sons, whom he had brought up with so much of love and affection, were after his position in the party. Destiny does play a cruel game at times.'

Srikant then narrated them the story of how Deen Dayal had tried to blackmail him. His voice was slightly emotional when he narrated those tense moments when he was saved unexpectedly from that situation.

Pankaj asked Srikant, 'So, was that the reason why you took early retirement from politics?'

Srikant paused for a while and said in somewhat determined voice, 'Yes. I suddenly realized that I was playing with fire all the time. I was running after power all my life. In the process, I accepted corrupt practices. I never thought of what happens if I got caught . . . ! I think people these days take everything for granted. What surprises me is that even though people know what would happen if they are exposed, still they assume as if they are never going to get caught. It is like everyone knows that they are going to die, yet no one actually thinks of his death. They feel that it is still too distant, a long time away.'

Vikram said, 'Very true. It is said that before an accident happens, there would be a narrow escape at least 14 times. The only difference during those 14 times is that the situation was averted by a very narrow margin. Sometimes we realize how close we were and many times we do not. So, what do you propose to do next?'

Srikant said, 'I feel lucky that I got this realization so soon in my life. Actually it is not so soon, as I am already 60 but then, better late than never. I want to spend rest of my life guilt free. I do not want any more power. I want to lead a normal life. When I face someone on street, my conscious should be clear. There is nothing that I would want to hide. When I talk to my parents, I should be able to look in their eyes and speak. When I teach morality to my children, I do not want to sound like a hypocrite. People might say that, 'Sau chuhe khake billi haj ko chali. I don't care for that. I feel that now that I am reformed, I should lead a better life from this very moment.'

Everyone seemed to appreciate his thought process. Srikant appeared as though someone had removed a big burden from his head. He appeared relaxed and calm.

It was now Amit's turn.

He started off, 'Well guys, as you were aware, I had too much interest in doing business. I always wanted to be on my own. I did not want to have a boss. When you have a boss, there is automatically a cap on your creativity, because you only obey instructions. I had always dreamt of having my own cabin with an executive chair and classic paintings adoring the walls. It was such a pleasure to receive the guests in my office and see the hidden feelings of admiration in them. I was always lucky in my adventures. May be, it is true that God helps those who help themselves.'

Vikram said, 'Amit, which was the turning point in your life?'

Amit thought for a while and said, 'Yes, when I was the General Manager—Marketing in charge of the entire Indian operations, I started dreaming big. I felt that I was toiling day and night having sleepless nights worrying about meeting the sales targets, while the owner of the company was sleeping peacefully without making any visible efforts to reach the goals. This made me think. Why should I not work for myself? If I put in the same efforts for my own company, then I can earn much more than what I am earning now. These thoughts propelled me into action. As I had already developed my base in marketing network, I knew the markets and the ways to market a product. I knew the psyche of the customers, and had developed strategies to deal with dealers and distributors. Having grown in marketing of FMCG sector, I could sense the pulse of the market.'

Vikram interrupted, 'So, you started with a marketing setup?'

Amit said, 'First I took the distributorship for the products of company I worked for. Then I expanded my operations by taking marketing agency for the renowned FMCG for the western territory. I could surpass the targets almost every quarter as I employed the right people in my organization. You may not believe, but I personally interviewed each and every person recruited in my company. I believed that every employee was the brand ambassador for the company. All assets are measurable, but the human resources are intangible. A person employed for Rs. 25k per month can yield you a business worth either Rs. 50k per month or even Rs. 5k per month. It all depends on right selection and right environment to perform. The human potential is unlimited.'

Amit paused for a while, gestured at Vikram and continued, 'At times, I roped in Vikram to motivate my senior management team. And it worked wonders. After every training program, they would come back charged with energy and look forward to achieve every target defined for them. My job was to ensure that the motivation continued. That is why I empowered them to take decisions within their domain, delegated my responsibilities to a large extent and only looked after the end results. It may not work every time, but in my case, it worked wonderfully well.'

Pankaj said, 'We read in newspapers recently that you are big time into philanthropy now. How did this change happen?'

For the first time ever since he started talking about his past, his body language reflected traces of helplessness. He said, 'I was reaching new milestone with each of my new ventures. I had ventured into backward integration by manufacturing FMCG products in diversified areas. That significantly increased our profitability. The turning point for me was when my son returned from abroad after acquiring a management degree and refused to join my business. I was crestfallen. I had built this empire brick by brick hoping to proudly hand it over to my son and retire watching him increase it even further. But he politely informed me that my business did not interest him. I could have still pressurized him to join, but I knew that such an arrangement would not last long. He would have become a robot in my house or possibly run away. Neither of these was a preferred option. I wanted him to live his life enthusiastically, have goals in life, have the satisfaction of doing something worthwhile and lead a peaceful life.'

The atmosphere had turned a bit emotional as everyone empathized with Amit. It was a very difficult situation.

Amit said, 'Unfortunately, the generation gap is not only a gap in years but also in the ideologies and the attitudes. He had no value for my business. He respects me a lot, even today. He admires me for the efforts taken by me over the year to rise to this fame. Yet, he feels that he would not enjoy being a part of it. He was interested in Bollywood. Once I realized that no amount of persuasion would help him change his mind, I supported him in his endeavor. I felt sad that my dream of seeing my son take over the reins of business from me in my old age were going to remain unfulfilled. I suddenly felt a deep vacuum in my life. I started wondering, what was the purpose of doing all this. I have to call it a day sometime and if my own son does not takeover, am I doing all this for charity? It was a very painful phase, but once I accepted the reality, I got used to the facts of life. I made every effort to make him a success in the Bollywood. His first film was a huge success. That put him on cloud nine. However, life had some bitter lessons for him as his next two film bombed at the box office. Now he is firmly on ground, working hard, and hoping for a better future. The failure has taught him good lessons to be humble and the rare quality of accepting defeat gracefully.'

Srikant said, 'So, that was the trigger for philanthropic initiatives?'

Amit said, 'In a way yes. When my own son did not want to carry forward my legacy, I did not find any meaning in expanding my business empire further. However, major push for this came due to some trivial incidents in my life. Sometimes, very small and unassuming incidents spark off a new chapter in life to such an extent that you feel surprised later when you see the cause of it all. I still remember that particular day, when by sheer coincidence, I helped a begging boy on street, helped my driver's son to set up his own business and also received a group of representatives from a charity house who described their activities to me. I was suddenly seeing a new side of life. All along, I was making efforts for my own betterment. For my business, my family, my home, my assets . . . in short, everything associated with me. And I think majority of people in this world are in this category. They think about themselves much more than others. But if you really think of it, even animals live for themselves. There has to be a difference between human beings and animals, right?'

Amit looked at everyone, not exactly expecting an answer to his question, but to gauge their response to his thoughts.

Pankaj asked, 'Don't take it otherwise Amit, but you have been making money for a long time. Why this philanthropy now? I mean, the circumstances made you go the philanthropic way, and not the virtues of being philanthropic, correct?'

Amit thought for a while and answered, 'True. There are two main factors here. The first one is that you need to be rich for being philanthropic. You can't help others when you yourselves are in need. It is like the airline safety announcement which urges you to put the oxygen mask first on yourselves before attempting to help others. Unfortunately, more than 80% of the world population falls in this category. The second factor is that when you start earning money more than your requirements for survival as per your society standards, you slowly get financially independent. This phase is very critical in the sense it reflects a person's character. You would be amazed to see the widest options people would choose to spend the surplus money they have after meeting their basic necessities. Some would invest in shares and stocks, some invest in property, some spend it on holidaying around the world, some buy expensive designed clothes and accessories, some spend it in gambling and some acquire bad habits.'

Everyone was listening carefully to this businessman's take on spending habits of people with surplus money. They wondered whether he studied this behavior as a part of promoting some of his products.

Amit took a pause and then said, 'There is a stage beyond this. When a person earns so much money that even after lavishly spending on his habits there is still some surplus money left. It is at this stage that the people with good upbringing take to philanthropy. With due respect to all the philanthropists in the world, I say that they became philanthropists when they realize the stark truth of life that money cannot buy every happiness in this world. They are all in the twilight of their lives and feel too empty to realize that they have become rich while there are millions of poor people around them. Some of them feel guilty too, while actually they are not at fault at all. They became rich because of their efforts and have every right to become rich. I am also one of this category. Tomorrow when I leave this world, I want to go with a feeling that I was helpful to someone in need. I shall consider my life to be successful, if I was able to change the lives of some people for better than what it would have been otherwise.'

They all seemed to agree his frank views on philanthropy and philanthropic people in the world.

Amit said, 'Today, my trust goes around the villages in India and give free textbooks and notebooks to the poor meritorious students who cannot afford them. We take up the expenses of poor students who have cleared various competitive exams but cannot afford the fees of professional courses. We are tying up with various jails to identify the prisoners who were inside because they committed some crime due to circumstances but were actually good natured. We teach them skills to be self sufficient when they are released. I get immense satisfaction, if I am able to improve at least one life. It feels good to be good.'

There was a silence.

It was now Vikram's turn to share his past.

Vikram said, 'My life has been a kind of roller coaster. As you all would recall, I was considered the most 'clever' among four of us just because I secured a seat in engineering college at that time, while you all could not. But now, I realize that it was a wrong phenomenon to associate cleverness with the ability to fetch a seat in an engineering or medical college. What these entrance exams actually test are your skills in remembering large amount of data over a period of few months. Unfortunately, even today, the same sentiments are widely prevalent in our society.'

Everyone was surprised at such a frank opinion expressed by an engineer who took pride in those days for being called an engineer.

Vikram continued, 'Many times, I feel that an engineer's family is happier than him, because while he spends more time in the factory with the machines, his family enjoys the luxuries he has brought for their enjoyment. In my view, one of the worst slaveries in this world is found in the remote factories where the engineer has no life of his own. He earns money, but has no time and avenue to spend it. I pity the families of such engineers, who sacrifice city life just to be with him. Such companies do have townships, where one is forced to like whatever entertainment facilities are available there. But human mind is also very strange. When something is thrust upon it, it dislikes it.'

Everyone was surprised to know the feeling of an engineer about townships.

Vikram continued, 'Adding to the miseries, the steel factory which I joined was in commissioning stage. Oh my God, I still remember those days, when I used to spend almost 14 hours a day at the factory. It was as if, the outside world had ceased to exist for me. I did not read the newspaper for days together. I used to sleep like a log, tired from a hard day's work every night. I used to feel absolutely hopeless to wake up in the morning and head for the factory knowing well that I may not return till late night. I dread at the thought even now, when I think that I spent almost two years in this condition. I got so exhausted by this tiresome routine that I fell terribly sick one day and that is when I decided to change my profession. I wanted to live a life of my own. I needed some time for myself every day, to reinvent myself. You may earn millions of rupees, but if you have no time to spend it the way you want to, it is mere waste. People often forget that life is limited. It cannot be extended by any means. They need to get their priorities right in the first place. At least they need to implement a mid-course correction, whenever they realize that they are not truly enjoying life. Life is not meant to be spent in hardship. It needs to be lived happily enjoying each and every moment.'

Vikram paused for a while to observe the expressions on everyone's face to check whether they were getting bored of his lecture or were absorbing what he said. He found that they were indeed listening to him very carefully.

Vikram continued, 'It was while I was in hospital that I came across some self-help books and after reading them, decided to change my profession. I wanted to spread the knowledge of self potential to as many people as possible. I wanted people to identify their passion and pursue them so that they can enjoy life while simultaneously working. I have observed in subsequent years that unfortunately, there are too many people in this world who are in wrong profession. For these people, life is a big challenge to be faced every day. They have long forgotten the simple pleasures of life, such as appreciation from seniors at the workplace, self contentment, rewards for good performance etc. They slog every day to better their performance, but they cannot, because their heart is not in that job. And anything which is not done straight from the heart does not produce good results. Through my programs I started urging people to listen to their mind as well as heart. They deserve a better life.'

Pankaj interrupted, 'So, your focus was only on those misfits? What about those who were in the profession of their liking?'

Vikram said, 'Of course, for those who were in right profession, I enabled them to unleash their true potential and achieve far superior results in their work and personal life through systematic programs. That is how I gained fame around the world. And I started getting requests for doing programs from West, East and Middle East alike. I started travelling around the world. This was the profession, which I liked so much that I was getting a kind of kick after my every lecture or a session. It gave me too much of pleasure to see people benefitting from my presentations. And this is where I made the biggest mistake of my life, for which I regret even now . . .'

Everyone was stunned and wondered what it could be.

Vikram said, 'I was slowly getting drifted away from my sweet heart, Vineetha. I think I took her for granted. I never really bothered to look into her mind and know her likes and dislikes, her feelings and emotions. This cost me heavily. I lost her . . . forever.'

Vikram's voice suddenly choked with emotions. His eyes became wet.

He composed himself and continued, 'I went around improving others lives, but failed to notice that my own life was sinking slowly. She even told me one day before she was diagnosed with cancer that we needed to spend more time together. I should have listened to her then. Maybe she had an inkling of the things to come in near future. I took her lightly. Nevertheless, I am happy that ever since she was diagnosed with cancer, I cancelled all my appointments and spent as much time with her as possible. And I was too amazed to see how she had gathered a high degree of knowledge on philosophy. I think she used to read all my treasure while I was away, to pass time. And that really helped her to take the calamity with so much ease. I learnt a lot of things from her during her last few days. She was a gem.'

Vikram again paused just to be more composed. He said, 'I was totally shattered after her death. I felt as if there was no meaning in life. Many times I contemplated committing suicide. I read lot of philosophical books during those days and learnt the essence of life. I have come in this world without my consent. I shall go from here without my consent. While god has given us the freedom to a certain degree on what we can do, the entry and exit pass for each one of us are still signed by him. Without his signature, we cannot enter or leave this world. We need to spend the time allocated to us, whether we like it or not. We feel that death is painful, but you would be surprised to know that for some people, death is a far more preferred option than the painful life they live. One can't help it.'

'I took long time to recover and then started a cancer hospital to treat the poor people free of cost. That was the minimum I could do in remembrance of Vineetha. I feel happy today, to see that many poor people from across the country come to our hospital for free treatment. I started spending my time on imbibing good values in people by giving them some devotional and spiritual talks in the evening in a nearby temple. Now I have no more feelings left for me. I am a 'Sthita Pradnya' as described in Bhagwad Gita. I take life as it comes. I do not get too happy or too sad at anything.'

Now it was Pankaj's turn to speak.

Pankaj said, 'I am feeling so happy today for you guys coming to my village and spending some time with me. As children, we used to spend lot of time together. We played together, we quarreled and also studied together. However, the time drifted us apart and life took us on different paths. I thank god that he presented us this opportunity that we all meet today and dwell in the past for few moments. Few people in this world are so fortunate as to be able to meet their good childhood friends in their sixties.'

Pankaj's happiness was not just in words, but was also seen in his body language and facial expressions.

He continued, 'After graduation, I had an average job in a private company. I was struggling to meet the needs and spending money only on necessities. It was then that I realized that I had this exceptional gift of teaching. As I was good in maths, I took up tuitions to support my family. And it flourished in no time. I was a successful tutor within my locality and was running to full capacity. I took new space for tuitions and expanded further. At one point I gave up my job, as my income from tuitions far exceeded my salary. All was going well, when one day I realized that I was selling education at a price. It was not correct. Knowledge is priceless. One who has it is blessed person. It then becomes his moral duty and social obligation to transmit it to others. With these thoughts, I decided to stop this money making business called coaching centre and came to Shantinagar to help the people here.'

Vikram intervened, 'Any specific reason to choose Shantinagar?'

Pankaj said, 'Well, no specific reason. It was just that I wanted to be among people who are deprived of the educational facilities and to improve their lives with proper education. When I came here, I knew that it was a big task I had undertaken. The results would be very far away to measure and quantify them against the efforts gone in making them. It was like planting a seed and expecting fruits. The tree needs continuous attention and caring to grow up and bear fruits. Today I am happy that I have reaped plenty of fruits of my efforts. My students are today spread around the world and in good positions. More than just making them literates, I made them educated citizens. They are conscious of their responsibilities towards the society and country they are from. They know what is good and what is bad for them. They are god fearing people who will pass on this goodness to their future generations to come.'

Pankaj paused for a while and then continued, 'There is one more small reason to choose this village. My grandfather hailed from this village before he came to Mumbai and settled there in his young age. So, I needed to repay some of my 'moral loan' to this place by doing something good for the people of Shantinagar. And I am happy today to see that I have succeeded in my endeavor. There are thousands of small villages in India. It is not practically possible for me to go and stay in each and every village and try to educate its people. But I am sure, there are many more Pankaj's created by almighty who will take care of the rest of villages at appropriate times.'

Amit remarked, 'But we read in some newspapers that you have also brought lot of awareness among the villagers in water harvesting, solar energy, sustainability etc . . . !'

Pankaj said, 'Oh yes. That is the need of the hour. Unfortunately, today the people behave as though environmental problems do not belong to them; they feel that these are somebody else's problems. This is not correct. All of us live in the same environment. The earthquakes and floods do not differentiate between rich and poor. For the sea levels rising due to the global warming, everybody on the coast is same. And this is not the problem only with people; even some rich nations have this attitude. They want poor countries to control the carbon emissions and in lieu get the license to waste energy in a luxurious way. So, again I did my bit about bringing awareness in Shantinagar. I am proud that every drop of rain water is accounted for in this village and every unit of electricity is spent judiciously.'

Srikant said, 'But Pankaj, your son is settled in USA. Why don't you too go and live there?'

Pankaj thought for a while and said, 'Srikant, I do agree that I need to stay with my son in my old age, but I am only sixty now. Still I have stamina and will power to stay on my own with my wife. All these villagers are like my brothers and sisters. Yes, I do sometimes feel that my son should have been with me. But then, he has a different life to lead and I have my own. We respect each other's spheres of life and do not intervene in them. Nevertheless, I am happy and proud that my son still respects me a lot and does not disobey my instructions. I have seen the miseries of people when their children do not respect them. You might conquer the whole world, but if your children do not look up to you with respect, you feel absolutely bad. I consider them the poorest of poor.'

Vikram said, 'So, what next Pankaj?'

Pankaj took a deep breath and said, 'See Vikram, we all are here on this earth for few years. We come and go. We leave behind the imprints of our actions, which are defined by our character and deeds. I wish to spend my remaining life in Shantinagar. Because this is what gives me happiness and this is my passion. Ultimately what counts is 'how' you lived your life and not 'how long' . . . Life has been very kind to me so far. I wish it continues to be so in future too.'

*   *   *

That night the four of them slept in the front yard of the house on beds woven from jute threads. The cool breeze was flowing through, making the environment very pleasant. Amit and Srikant could vouch that the freshness in air was far superior to the high quality air conditioners in their homes. The Moon was shining brightly directly overhead hiding momentarily behind the white clouds. The same moon was appearing in the sky since their childhood. And the same moon would continue to appear long after they would have gone.

Vikram sometimes wondered the ultimate purpose of life. Why did people appear on this earth? From where they came and where they would go after this? The space extended far beyond this earth and even much beyond the so-called solar system. So, did it really matter to the creator whether people existed on this planet or ceased to exist one day? If tomorrow the entire mankind on earth is wiped out, would the sun still continue to rise in the east? Obviously yes. Then, is this entire setup designed for someone else? Was the creation of mankind on this earth accidental in nature? Does the creator know that we are living here with all our feelings and emotions or he is simply oblivious of even our presence at all?

When was the beginning and when is the end of this existence? What happened before that and what would happen after this? When one thinks of these things, one feels humbled. Yet people on this earth spend their lifetimes in blindly going after money, estate, bank balance etc. When one looks at such things from this higher plane, it appears almost childish if not ridiculous. When everyone knows perfectly well that they are not going to carry anything with them, why do people still crave to amass the material wealth?

Why are there so many sufferings in this world? Why can't we envisage a world where everyone is happy and satisfied? Why is the creator giving some liberty of thought to the people, by which they commit crimes and then suffer later? Does the creator get some sort of pleasure in making people suffer and watch their sufferings from above? Is it noble for him to do so?

They all were relaxed after meeting one another after so many years and in such good moods. They all had experienced lot of thrills and anxieties in their respective lives. Now, in their sixties, life was apparently going soft on them in terms of giving any more challenges. They all had lived their lives very well. They tasted the power in different fields. They took the responsibilities associated with those powers. They were successful in some of their attempts and had also experienced failures.

They had also realized that life will not always be exactly the way one desires it to be. There is some control always left with god, who exercises it at his discretion and circumstances. While one may assume lot of power in this world, sometimes life too plays games with people.

The power games of life . . . .